THE WITCH of the WAVE.

LONDON : W. S. JOHNSON, 60, ST. MARTIN'S LANE, CHARING CROSS.

TO BE HAD OF ALL BOOKSELLERS.

No. 1.

THE WITCH OF THE WAVE.

CHAPTER I.

THE BRIGANTINE.

IT was a fine, mild evening in the month of September, 1814, that we open our story. The rich glories of sunset were fast deepening into the sober twilight, to be succeeded by the still more sombre shades of night. It was just at the lovely twilight hour of this fair autumnal eve—just as day was verging into night, that a small brigantine, of a most beautiful model, and exceedingly rakish appearance, came to anchor in the harbor of Boston, off Copp's Hill. Her appearance, as she lay almost motionless upon the waves, from above which her long, low hull seemed scarcely to rise, was to the eye of one accustomed to the sea, beautiful and bewitching in the extreme.

She was of about one hundred and fifty tons burden, clipper-built, and of unusual beauty of appearance, and as she rocked gently upon the undulating waves, seemed proudly conscious of her beauty; surpassing greatly that of any craft upon the waters around her. Her hull was white, relieved by two very narrow ribbons of red and blue, of scarcely two inches in width, and the same distance separating the two colors, the red above.

Her deck was of a blood-red hue, relieved by the color of the hatch and companion-ways, which were of light green, as also the bulwarks, save the ports, which were painted black, and now closed. She carried ten brass twelve-pounders, of as bright and clear a polish as could be imparted to that metal. Their carriages were of the same hue as the deck. Besides these, she carried a-midships a long thirty-two pounder mounted on a pivot, and easily brought to bear at any point; it was painted black, and bore the name of "Tormentor."

The masts of the brigantine were exceedingly lofty and rakish, tapering almost to reeds, and, with the yards, were white as the driven snow. At a distance, with all sails set, the brigantine would have been mistaken for a white cloud; and upon nearer inspection the mistake would prove to be no mistake, for that was her name. The "White Cloud" was the name of the brigantine we have described; a privateer, and just returned from a cruise as our story opens.

The crew of the brigantine, numbering in all eighty men, were assembled upon deck; a portion of them young and noble-looking fellows, but the majority of them were a fierce, brutal-looking set of men, in whose faces evil was predominant. As the privateer came to anchor, a loud cheer burst from the former portion of the crew, which was re-echoed by hundreds upon shore, and from the numerous craft in the bay. A second cheer swelled loudly out upon the air, when, ere it had died away, a loud, stern voice commanded "Silence!" and at the moment a man sprung from up the companion-way, with a pistol clutched tightly in his grasp. He was a heavily-built young man, rather above the middle stature, with a fierce and evil expression upon his countenance. There were evident signs that his face was once possessed of beauty; but vice and dissipation, which were plainly visible to the eye, and a perfect abandonment to every evil passion, had nearly obliterated every mark of former beauty. He cast a fierce glance towards the group of young sailors as he strode toward them. But neither his command nor his appearance was regarded, and another loud and hearty cheer burst upon the air.

"Silence, I say!" thundered again the Captain, in a tone of fiercest rage. "Silence! or by Heaven I'll shoot the first who dares to raise his voice again! We shall have the whole town aboard of us; and I swear I'll not be boarded while the brigantine lies in these waters!"

For a moment there was silence upon the deck of the privateer; when from among the crew stepped forth a young and fearless-looking sailor, and in a bold voice he said, "I dare to break the silence you have commanded, and fear not your threat of violence. My comrades and myself no longer acknowledge your authority as Captain of the "White Cloud." You have forfeited all right and title to the command of this vessel or its crew, by a deed that will bring you and the greater portion of those around you, as base and wicked as yourself, to justice, and an ignominious and well-merited death. You have braved your own fate by running into this harbor, for ere to-morrow's sun shall rise, you and a score of your basest myrmidons will be incarcerated within the walls of a prison. I swore, as we all swore, to keep the secret of the hellish piracy you committed against a foreign flag, and also against the flag which now waves above. I did not swear because I feared to die, but that some day or other I might bring you to justice. This urged me to take the oath. Ere twenty-four hours, I hope to see you delivered up to justice, and to free from a thraldom worse than death a fair being who suffers the most cruel captivity below."

The face of the Captain had somewhat paled at the bold and fearless words of the young seaman, but it was not fear, but pent-up rage. His brow was contracted into a terrible frown, and there was a fearful expression upon his face, and a fearful smile upon his lips, as he gazed upon him who so boldly dared to confront him, and so openly denounced him. His face slightly twitched, and his finger played nervously upon the trigger of the pistol he clutched in his hand. For a moment he gazed upon the young seaman, and then in a voice calm and sarcastic, he said—

"I thank you, most heartily indeed, for informing me thus early of your amiable intentions, that I may thwart them. By all the powers of darkness!" he uttered in a fiercer tone, "*you* shall never betray me! You shall keep the oath you swore; the secret shall never be uttered by you, if death can seal your lips!"

He levelled his pistol at the breast of the undaunted seaman, and pulled the trigger; it flashed, but missed fire. With an oath of disappointment he hurled the weapon with fearful force at his intended victim. But he was doomed to be twice foiled; it went by its intended mark, taking off the hat of the young man, and whirling through the air fell into the water some distance from the brigantine. Quicker than thought, after his miraculous escape from the death that menaced him, the young sailor sprung toward the murderous Captain, and struck him a heavy blow in the face, which felled him like an ox to the deck. The blow stunned him, but only for an instant. He sprung up, his face streaming with his hot blood, and in a voice of maddened fury, cried—

"Seize him! bind him, quickly!" and he himself sprung toward him, as did a dozen others. But quicker than they, the young seaman sprung from them, and with the bound of a tiger he leaped over the bulwarks into the water, and disappeared beneath its surface. The Captain uttered an oath in a voice of hellish rage and disappointment, at being thrice foiled.

"He snatched a pistol from the belt of a seaman near him and sprung towards the bulwark. All were now gazing over the side of the vessel from which the fearless young sailor had leaped, but no appearance of him was to be seen. Darkness, which was now fast settling upon the water, would soon prevent objects of the size of a man's head from being seen much distant from the vessel.

With straining eyes the Captain looked around upon the water in search of his intended victim. But nothing could be discerned above the surface indicating in the least the appearance of a man's head.

"By all the fiends, if he escapes, the brigantine must leave these waters, and sooner than I wished," said the Captain, in a tone of fierce vexation. "But—ah! what is that?" he exclaimed suddenly, to himself, directing his eyes toward a small dark object upon the water, nearly astern of the vessel, within pistol shot. He levelled the pistol at the object he had discovered and fired, ere any other upon the vessel's deck was aware of his intention.

The report of the pistol rung out loud and sharp upon the water, and all eyes were now turned in the direction he had fired. At that instant the dark object which had been the mark of the Captain rose up from the water, discovering what appeared to be in the indistinct twilight the head and arms of a man, struggling as if in the agonies of death. The struggles were but momentary, and the unfortunate victim sunk down from sight in a moment after. All eyes eagerly watched for his re-appearance, but there was no sight of him again. All were aware who it was that had perished before their sight—the victim of the inhuman act of the Captain—but there was no word uttered by one of that crew.

"He'll tell no tale now, I'll be sworn," said the Captain, as he threw his pistol to the deck. "Yet I'll be sure," he said, as if yet in doubt of his victim's fate.

Ordering a boat to be lowered alongside, and manned, which order was quickly obeyed, and speaking a few words in an under tone to a fierce and ruffianly-looking seaman, he jumped in at the bows and pushed the boat from the vessel.

The seaman to whom he had spoken was a powerful and savage-looking fellow, and as the boat pushed off, he approached and spoke in a low tone of voice to several of the crew, as savage-looking as himself, and who seemed to assent to what he said.

There was a sudden movement among them, and in a moment more a general scuffle ensued upon the deck of the brigantine. It lasted but a few moments, in which short space of time a dozen men were bound and thrown to the deck. It was now too dark to distinguish who they were, and they were gagged to prevent any outcry.

In a few moments the bound seamen were all taken from the deck down into the hold, and left, gagged as they were, in the darkness.

All was now still and silent as the night upon the deck of the brigantine, where but a few moments before the murderous and mysterious scenes were enacted which we have detailed to the reader. It was half an hour after the boat had left the vessel that she returned. As the Captain touched the deck, he called the name of Mardon.

"Ay, ay," was the response returned, and in a moment he was joined by the ruffian he had spoken to as he left the vessel.

"Have you done as I directed, Mardon? have you secured them?"

"Yes, they are below, bound and gagged," answered he.

"That's well, but they must not remain here, Mardon; we shall be boarded in the morning by the owners of the brigantine! We must get them ashore to-night, and keep them out of sight till we sail. As for that young Warner, he'll give us no further trouble; he's safe in Davy Jones' locker! That shot settled his accounts!"

Thus spoke the Captain of the brigantine as lightly of the deed he had committed, as one would of the most trifling affair of an every-day occurrence.

"But I must go ashore and see old Redskin; perhaps he can stow away these chicken-hearts below, for a few days. We *must* fix things all right before morning! The owners will be aboard then, and everything must appear as it ought to their eyes. Its my opinion, Mardon, that this war will not last much longer; then our commission's up. It has been partly a privateer's and partly a free commission; and by Heaven, I should hate to resign the brigantine, and surrender the *free* commission! What say you, Mardon?"

"I am of your mind exactly, Captain," answered Mardon. "I like the free commission; its get what you can, and keep what you get, and no allowance for owners."

"And the others, Mardon?"

"They're all right, Captain; every one would ship under the free flag, I'll be sworn; and the quicker we hoist it the better. But, Captain, what the devil shall we do with those fellows below?"

"I'll manage that, if we can get them ashore to-night, into the care of old Redskin; he'll keep them safe enough. I have an old account to settle with him, and I'll cancel it before I sail! He thinks its forgot and forgiven, but I'll remind him of it! But I'll go, and be back in an hour. Its devilish dark, and that will favor us the more in getting those fellows ashore."

As he said this, the Captain got into the boat and shoved off. The rollicking of the oars was heard for a few moments, then died away in the distance.

The boat went swiftly through the water in the darkness, and soon touched at a pier, at which the Captain ascended by means of small blocks of wood fastened to one of the piles. Ordering his men to wait for him, he walked rapidly up the pier, like one familiar with the place. It was nearly ten o'clock, and the part of the town in which he now was was dark and deserted. He passed rapidly on his way till he came at length to a street that intersected the pier; he turned into the street at the left, and passed on at the same quiet pace over the wretched walk. It was a quarter of the town where dwelt the lowest and vilest of the population. Rays of light streamed into the street from the open doors and windows of the miserable hovels, and the sounds of drunken, boisterous mirth came forth from the lowest dens of iniquity. The night was mild, and squads of half drunken sailors and miserable females were collected around the doors of the numerous dram-shops; some cursing and swearing, some laughing and singing ribald songs, while others, too drunk, lay sprawling upon the pavement, there to lie till sleep restored their senses. Scores of these miserable creatures the privateer Captain passed, as he pursued his way along the streets—some standing, some sitting, and some lying upon the ground. Once, as he passed the door of the lowest tavern in the vicinity, a poor drunken sailor was ejected therefrom by the proprietor of the establishment, and with a kick, accompanied with an oath, sent headlong into the street. Such were the scenes the Captain witnessed as he passed unheedingly on, as if familiar and accustomed to the like.

He at length slackened his rapid pace, and stopped before the door of a drinking shop, over which was suspended a sign, on which was represented an anchor, and had it been in the day-time a close scrutiny would have discovered to the eye the words "Best Bower."

"This is it, and there's Mike himself," said the privateer Captain, as he stepped in at the door.

It was a low, filthy place, dimly lighted by two or three lamps, the flickering and unsteady lights of which could be scarcely seen through the clouds of smoke that filled the place from the pipes of a dozen smokers, who were ranged together upon an old settee that once claimed a back and arms, but was now minus these unnecessary parts, as the settee was placed against a partition, thus affording a back to the occupants. To the left of the door, at one end of the room, was a bar, behind which, upon two shelves, were arranged in tempting array, black junk bottles, each with a brass label thrown over the neck, indicating the different kinds of liquors contained within. A dirty tumbler, with an old dried lemon upon it, was placed between each bottle, completing the array.

At one end of the bar inside, was an individual of the most corpulent dimensions, resting with both elbows upon the filthy and blackened counter, his hands supporting his head, while from out his mouth issued volumes of dense smoke imbibed from a short pipe, black with long continued use.

His face was bloated, as it seemed, almost to bursting, and of a deep crimson hue that owed itself to a free and long continued use of brandy. His fleshy hands and wrists were of the same shining hue as his face. His hair was short, and fiery red, and was in good contrast with the hue of his face. His eyes were small, of hazel hue, and were now fixed upon the counter, as if in thought, or as if some deep calculation was revolving in his mind. So deep was his reverie, that he noticed not the entrance of the new comer, the privateer Captain, who walked up to the bar, and gave him a hearty slap upon the shoulder, which broke his thoughtful trance.

"Mike, what the devil are you thinking of?" exclaimed the Captain, laughing at the astonished, and now upright mass of flesh before him, who stood regarding him with looks that seemed to imply that he was somewhat over-familiar with his shoulders, and rather too hearty in his greeting.

"How are you, old boy?—give us your flipper, Mike. What! you don't know me? Has one year altered me so, that Mike Marshall has forgotten me? Come, let's drink, old boy! perhaps a little whiskey will quicken your memory," said the Captain, laughing.

There was a sudden expression that lighted up the countenance of the fat man as the Captain spoke this, as if the mere mention of whiskey had started his somewhat flagging memory.

Taking the short black pipe from his mouth, and with a chuckling laugh that puffed a cloud of smoke full into the face of the man before him, he exclaimed, in a voice soft and effeminate—

"Captain Wing, I vow!" and reaching forth his hand, it was grasped in the brawny one of the Captain with a gripe so vice-like, that it started the tears in the eyes of Mike, who uttered an exclamation of pain, and withdrew it, squeezed almost into one mass of flesh half its original size. Rubbing his compressed hand with the other till it had become somewhat restored to its former shape, and while his face worked with all sorts of expressions, he exclaimed, in a half laughing, half crying tone—

"That was a hard squeeze, though, Captain! Shake hands with the devil, before I will with you again!"

"I fancy he will," said the Captain to himself, turning half round to eject a quid of tobacco from his mouth, replacing it by another fresh quid.

"But I vow, Captain, who'd a thought o' seeing you? Didn't hear the "White Cloud" had got in—

when d'ye arrive?—what luck have ye had?" and as Mike asked these questions, he placed a bottle of whiskey and a couple of tumblers upon the bar.

"Got in to-night, Mike," said the Captain, as he half filled the tumbler with whiskey. "No luck at all—privateering aint worth following. But come, let's drink; and then I've some matters to talk of in privacy with you, Mike."

Mike filled a tumbler with brandy, and the two drank to each other's good luck.

"Now, Mike, I must have some talk in private with you, in the back room. Is it vacant?"

"Yes, here's a light; you can enter, and I'll follow you soon."

The Captain took the lamp, and passed through a door at one end of the bar, leading into a small, dark apartment, containing a table and two or three ricketty chairs.

"Be quick, Mike, for I'm in a hurry," he said, as he passed into the room.

"In a moment, Captain. Here, Jake, come here: take my place while I talk with the Captain, in the back room."

Jake answered the summons, and seated himself upon an old stool inside the bar, with a face as grave as a parson's. He was sitting upon the old settee smoking his pipe in silence when the host of the "Best Bower" called to him, and had probably held the important station he now held before. He cast a look towards the others upon the settee, as if vain of the confidence reposed in him by the landlord, who, after cautioning him not to taste a drop, or credit a glass to any one, passed into the little back room, and closing the door, seated himself by the Captain.

"Can any one overhear us, Mike?"

"Not a word, Captain."

"Well, then, Mike, to the point at once. I'm in a fix, and you must help me out of it."

"A bad fix, hey! Well, what is it? I'll help an old friend, if I can. Rather scarce times for money now—business aint very lively—"

"It's nothing of that sort, Mike," said the Captain, who took the meaning of his avaricious companion. "It is'nt a pecuniary assistance I ask of you."

Mike breathed freer at these words, and rubbing his hands, said—

"No, no, Captain, I didn't suppose it was. In case it was, Mike Marshall's not the man to refuse you, you well know."

"I'm well sensible of that, Mike," said the Captain, in a tone of mock earnestness.

"But, Captain, what is this trouble? What's the fix you're in? Let's know, and if I can help you out of it, depend on't I'll do it."

"Well, Mike, I'll tell you; but first, its to be a secret between us, you understand—lisp it to no one."

"I swear eternal secrecy, Captain," said Mike, instantly.

"That's as long as I snal want you to keep the secret. But first tell me, Mike, if you can hide for a day or two, while I lay in port, a dozen men; so that they shall not be seen or heard?"

"Hide a dozen men! What the devil's in the wind, Captain?" exclaimed Mike, in a tone of surprise, as he stared at the Captain.

"Can you do it, Mike? Can you hide a dozen men, as I said before? You have the cellar now?"

"Yes."

"Then you can do it, Mike, and must."

This was uttered in a tone that implied a resolute will.

"Mike, I'll tell you all about it. I had some trouble with a fellow to-night, just after we came to anchor; he refused to obey my orders, as Captain of the "White Cloud,"—openly and flatly refused to obey my command, and defied my authority. We had some words, and he struck me to the deck; the blow stunned me and cut a slight gash upon my forehead. I jumped up in a moment, and levelled a pistol at him, and would have shot him, but it missed fire, and he jumped overboard to escape me. I saw him as he came up to breathe, and shot him in the water. There were a dozen who swore I struck him first, and swore that I should hang for his murder. I know I should be acquitted by any jury, but I could not wait for tardy justice to pronounce me guiltless, and so took the best means in my power to prevent my having to undergo a public trial, delayed for a year perhaps. I had these twelve men seized and bound, and they are now in the hold of the brigantine. But as the owners will be aboard in the morning, they must be removed to-night; and, Mike, your cellar must be the place to hide them. This is what brought me here to-night; you know what I want of you. What say you, will you hide these men till I sail?"

"A dozen men—how many days shall you lay in port, Captain?"

"Perhaps a week."

"Its a mighty risk to run, Captain, to have a dozen men in my cellar a week, as prisoners; if it should get out any how, why I vow, I should be jugged for life; I vow its a devilish risky job. I wont have anything to do with it, Captain."

"You wont, eh! but you must, old Redskin, and there's no getting away from it. You love money; you shall be paid well: how's that?"

"How much?" quickly asked Mike.

"I'll give you one hundred dollars to keep them a week, or if I only lay here one day, the same. What say you?"

"One hundred dollars—twelve of them—keep 'em a week. Its not enough, Captain Wing; its a great risk to run; my reputation is in danger—its not enough—I'll have nothing to do with it at any rate."

The Captain watched him—he knew he had not offered him enough, and he also knew there would be no scruples if he offered enough, notwithstanding Mike's assertion that he would have nothing to do with it at any rate.

"I'll give you two hundred, Mike."

"No."

"I'll give you three."

"No, Captain Wing. I tell you I'll have nothing to do with it; tempt me no more."

"I'll give you five hundred dollars, Marshall."

"Five hundred dollars, five hundred—twelve of them in my cellar—for a week—perhaps only one day—let me see—yes—I'll do it Captain, seeing its you in this bad scrape. Its on account of old friendship, Captain—nothing else."

"Its nothing else, I am well aware, Mike, that prompts you thus to help me out of the hazardous situation I am placed in; and I hope, Mike, that I shall be able to cancel the obligation you place me under to you, by your disinterestedness. I'll remember it, depend on 't."

The Captain uttered these words in a significant tone, and an expression of singular meaning passed over his face.

"Wholly on account of old friendship, Captain; nothing else would tempt me to undergo such a risk," said fat Mike again, as if he would impress upon the Captain's mind how sincere was his disinterested friendship for him.

"Certainly, Mike, I consider it so; but at what hour do you close? it's now eleven."

"Generally at twelve, Captain; I keep good hours. Some, less respectable, round here, are open till one."

"We must wait then till all are closed—about two o'clock, Mike, will be the hour; there will be no one about at that time. Have the trap open and the passage clear, so as not to hinder. We shall have to come twice with the fellows. Leave your door unlocked, and have a light at hand, Mike. I'll be off now; at two o'clock I'll be here again."

The Captain rose as he spoke, and made towards the door, when Mike spoke—

"But the money—"

"Shall be paid when the fellows are safe under the hatches," said the Captain, who anticipated what Mike intended to say. "Remember, Mike, your oath of secrecy; you have me wholly in your power; you can save, or ruin me."

"Not a word, Captain, I'm mum as a stone."

"You know Mike Marshall too well to doubt him."

"I do, Mike, too well to doubt your honor," said the Captain, in a tone that implied he knew the man with whom he had to deal.

"I'd not 'peach 'gainst an old friend, Captain, for ten times five hundred dollars," said Mike, in the tone of one who had a great and inviolable regard for honor.

Hang me, if I believe you will, old honesty, after I whisper in your ear what I know of you," said the Captain, in an under tone to himself, as he turned to leave the place.

"Let me get the five hundred dollars in my hands; then I'll square accounts with you," whispered Mike to himself, as the Captain left, after telling him to be ready when he arrived.

"I'll be ready for you," answered Mike. "Yes, I'll be ready for him," he said again to himself, as now alone he rubbed his hands, and chuckled with seeming satisfaction. "I have got him sure enough in my power; and he'll find how honest I am, with honest men like him. I'll set the fellows free, and have him where he wont see daylight till the noose is round his neck. It's all fol-de-rol what he told me; b'lieve he murdered him in cold blood; and now wants me to run a devil of a risk to save his neck. Humph!" ejaculated fat Mike. "I'd tie the rope myself. Curse me, but I b'lieve he'd as soon go pirating as privateering; but he wont leave this port again. I've got him and I'll have my revenge of

him. No, no, Will Wing, I haven't forgot *that* of you; and when you hang I'll tell you of it."

Mike muttered this in a somewhat savage tone; and as if perfectly confident that his friend would come to the ignominious end he spoke of.

He passed into the outer apartment; the Captain had gone, and the place, with the exception of Mike and the one who had filled the important station behind the bar during his absence, was vacant.

"Drank anything, Jake?" asked Mike, looking hard at the fellow, who sat perched upon the stool, looking as demure as a young judge.

"No, I aint," answered he.

"Sold any?" inquired Mike, as he pulled a small drawer out from before him.

"Nine glasses," drawled out Jake.

"Trust any?"

"No."

"That's all right," said Mike, in a very satisfied tone. "It's about twelve, shan't sell any more to-night. Close up, I guess; throw to the shutter, Jake, as you go out. Good night."

In a few moments the tap-room of the Best Bower was closed to all business for that night.

CHAPTER II.

THE CAPTAIN.

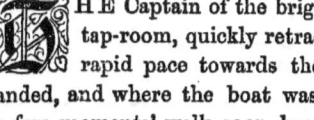HE Captain of the brigantine, as he left the tap-room, quickly retraced his steps with a rapid pace towards the pier where he had landed, and where the boat was in waiting for him. A few moments' walk soon brought him there, and, jumping from the pier into the boat, as it was now high water, seated himself in the stern sheets, and the next moment the boat shot rapidly from the pier over the dark water towards the brigantine.

A few moments' sharp rowing brought her within sight, as she lay at anchor, her long and now dark hull crouching low upon the water, like a sleeping leopard, before them. A moment more, and the boat lay alongside.

"Well," said Mardon, who was mate of the "White Cloud," in a tone of inquiry, as the Captain appeared on deck, "will old Redskin take care of these fellows, Captain?" he asked, in a tone of the utmost familiarity.

"Yes, I made a bargain with the old fiend, to keep them as long as we lay here, for five hundred dollars," answered the Captain.

"W-h-e-w!" whistled the mate. "That's a price, though, Captain; but you don't intend to give him that?"

"That's the bargain. I should have offered him a thousand, if five hundred would not have done, Mardon."

"I'd sooner take them down the harbor ten miles, and sink them, with a shot tied to each, to the bottom of the bay, rather than give him that price to hide them," said the worthy mate of the "White Cloud," as if in anger at the bargain of the Captain. "Curse me! but he'll make more money by this job than I have since I've been privateering!" said Mardon, in a harsh, dissatisfied tone.

"Well, well, Mardon, you need not growl about it; the bargain's made, and what's done is done," said the Captain, in a quick and impetuous voice. "But as to the five hundred dollars, that need not worry you: I'll settle with old Redskin. I have an old account against him for any amount, and I will square it with him before I go another cruise, and have what I mean to have—revenge. Only let me get these fellows into his care and keeping; I'll fix him then; and as to the money, he wont ask for't but once. But I never hinted to you, Mardon, before to-night, that Marshall was anything but my friend; that I nourished hate the deadliest, and have sworn revenge against him."

"No; I always supposed you were friendly," said the mate.

"Well, I will tell you; but step aft by the lights, I must see how the time goes on."

The two walked aft, and the Captain pulled from his fob a heavy-cased gold repeater, by which he saw it was about midnight. He returned the watch to its fob, and lighting a cigar, was about to speak, when Mardon asked of him what time he meant to take the bound seamen in the hold ashore?

"Between one and two," answered the Captain. "We must wait till the way is clear of stragglers, that might be curious to know what was going on. But now for what I was going to say to you in reference to Marshall and myself.

"He and I were once friends—shipmates together in the Chesapeake. There was a middy aboard of her, by the name of Burton, who was once a fellow-student of mine—a vain, conceited son of an aristocrat. He came on board the same time Marshall and myself shipped. A mutual dislike we had formed for each other at college, upon the decks of a man-of-war soon on my part grew to absolute hatred. I had shipped hastily, for certain reasons, as a common seaman; he came aboard as a middy, laced up in his uniform of blue, and looked as he trod the deck as if he had just come from his mother's drawing-room, and that the smell of tar was hardly endurable to his delicate and sensitive nerves, and a seaman was entirely beneath his notice. By degrees he became accustomed to the deck of a vessel, and then the petty authority of a middy began to display itself in numberless acts of a mean, contemptible nature. It was three days after he came aboard before he saw me, and then I purposely put myself in his way. He started with surprise, looked at me a moment, and then, with a look of contempt, he turned on his heel and walked away.

"I have never forgot the sneer nor the smile of scorn he gave me, as he drew his puny form to its full proportions, with the air of one who considered himself in every point my superior. That he was pleased to see me there in a station beneath him, I knew full well. I believed he would let no opportunity escape him to annoy me, by the exercise of his petty authority as a mid; for when was there ever a mid but what in the eyes of a sailor was considered a contemptible and useless appurtenance to a man-of-war?

"We had been a week at sea, when one morning this Burton was walking arm-in-arm with two mids, upon deck; I passed them and touched my hat to his two friends, but not to him. He felt the slight, and gave me a look, the meaning of which I understood as well as if he had spoken words. One hour afterwards I received a dozen lashes upon my back for this breach of respect towards Midshipman Burton.

"I swore I would have revenge for those lashes. I devised a scheme of revenge against Burton, and confided it to Marshall, and proposed to him to assist me in its execution. He refused. Like a fawning menial he had curried favor with the officers of the ship, and therefore would not listen to me.

"I executed it myself, much to the discomfiture of this Burton. A week afterwards, after the affair had blown over as I thought, I was seized up the gang-way, my back bared, and all hands piped to witness punishment. I was accused of being the perpetrator of the acts of malice against Burton; as I acknowledged it, I was sentenced to receive one hundred lashes which was executed.

"I received the one hundred lashes without a murmur, and had I been sentenced to be whipped till I cried for mercy, I would have died ere I would have uttered a word at the torture.

"As I was taken from the gangway, I fancied Burton was gazing at me, with looks of gratification at my disgrace. I looked at him for a moment; my brain was on fire; I felt the hot blood trickle down my back; revenge was the only thought within me; maddened and furious I sprang toward him, as an enraged tiger would upon its foe.

"So sudden, so unexpected, and so great the force I brought into action, that I bore him like a feather to the deck; I fell upon him; my hands sought his throat, an indescribable sensation whirled through my brain; I laughed wildly, but I remembered no more.

"I awoke one fair morning from what appeared to me a trance; I looked around, I was in my father's house. Surprised beyond measure at finding myself there, I attempted to rise from the bed on which I was lying, but found myself as helpless as an infant. How I came to be there, in my own chamber, helpless upon the bed, I could not conceive. I tried in vain to bring to my confused mind what occurrence had placed me there. My father soon after entered and came to my bedside. From him I learned that three weeks before I had been sent home from the frigate in a state of frenzy, and had remained so till this morning. The first question I asked of him was whether I had killed Burton. He answered me no; and that if I had I should not be accountable for the murder, on account of the madness that had seized me; he, as also all upon the deck of the frigate, supposing I was seized with this madness when I sprang at Burton.

"When I heard this, I swore an oath, that I would take the life of this man if ever I set my gaze upon him.

"But there was another upon whom I swore to wreak my vengeance, and that was Marshall. He had betrayed me, and it was to him I owed my punishment, and, Mardon, I know that of him, should I betray him, that would give the hangman a job. Tit for tat is fair, I suppose. If I *should* betray him, he'll hang as sure as I stand here.

"I'll be square with him ere I leave port; ha—ha! —Marshall little knows the rod I have in pickle for him."

The Captain laughed, as he spoke this, with evident satisfaction at the contemplated scheme of revenge he had in view.

It was half past one o'clock when he said to Mardon

WILL WING'S RETURN.

that it was time to be getting the bound seamen on deck. In a few moments they were taken from the hold, as he desired.

"Put six of them into the boat, Mardon, we shall have to go twice with them; see that the gags are sure, we must have no cries from the fellows."

Mardon proceeded instantly to execute the desire of the Captain, and in a moment or so, returned, saying the men were in the boat.

"They can make no noise?" said the Captain inquiringly.

"Not a breath, Captain," said the mate in answer.

"Well, six of us must go with them, Mardon; we must be armed in case anything should occur to interrupt us in our adventure. We must take cutlasses, for if we have anything to do, it must be done without much noise. Get me one; get one yourself, you will go with us; and see the others have them also. Quick, Mardon, get them into the boat."

As the Captain spoke he got over the side of the vessel into the boat, where lay the bound sailors, and in a moment he was followed by Mardon, and four others.

He pushed off, and the boat went silently and swiftly through the darkness, towards the pier where he had before touched that night, and which was soon reached. The boat was made fast, and the Captain, with Mardon, got upon the pier.

The bound seamen were now lifted, with some difficulty, out of the boat on to the pier.

"Cut the cords round their ancles, Mardon; they must walk, one with each of us."

This was soon done, and the prisoners stood upon their feet, with their arms pinioned behind them.

Wing now said, in a low voice, that no harm should come to them if they would walk along without any resistance, but threatened that if one refused to walk, he would run him through with his cutlass.

He then put his left arm through that of one of the seamen, which the rest did also; and ordering the strictest silence to be observed, he moved up the pier followed by the others. It was very dark, and the six couple, walking closely together, could not be seen, at a distance of ten feet. They proceeded upon their way, and soon came to the street.

Taking the middle, to avoid any stragglers that might happen to be abroad, they passed on in unbroken silence through the darkness.

A few moments' walk soon brought them in the vicinity of the tap-room of the Best Bower, without having encountered any one upon their way.

Wing soon found the door of the tap-room, by groping along by the side of the building; it was ajar, he pushed it open without noise and entered.

All was dark within, and the snoring of some person asleep broke the stillness.

"Mike! Mike!" he repeated, in a low, energetic tone, after waiting a few seconds in the dark.

"Holloa! Who's there?" exclaimed the voice of Mike a few moments after.

"It's me, Mike; strike a light, quick!" said he, impatiently.

"I've got one already, Captain," said Mike, with a yawn, and as he spoke a light streamed across the tap-room, from a dark lantern he held in his hand. He rose up from the settee, where he had been sleeping, and came toward the Captain.

"All here, Captain?" he asked, in a whisper.

"No; six of them. But come, lead the way to the cellar, Mike; we must dispose of these, and go for the rest. I want this job over."

"No sooner than I," said Mike, as he opened the lantern, and went toward a door at one end of the tap-room, opposite the bar. The door opened into a dark, narrow passage-way, which Mike turned into to the left, and proceeded along ten or twelve paces, followed by Wing and the others, to the passage, where a trap-door was raised up.

Mike held the lantern over the trap, and a pair of steps was seen, which descended to the cellar below. Down them the bound seamen were thrust, one after another, till the six were disposed of. The trap was then closed and fastened down strongly by an iron bar across it.

After seeing that it was secure, Mike and the others made their way back to the tap-room, from which Wing and his companions immediately departed, after saying that they should be back in half an hour.

"This is a d—d rascally piece o' business," he said, puffing forth a cloud of smoke from his mouth. "I vow he's a regular out-and-out pirate, this Wing. I'd like to know what he's up to. It's rascally to leave those chaps bound and gagged down in that cellar. I've a good mind to let 'em up, unbind 'em, and let 'em off, before he comes back with the others. I'll do it, I vow I will! I pity the poor fellows."

He started from the settee as he spoke his good intention, and taking up the lantern, went toward the door of the passage-way. He opened it, but shut it at the same moment.

"No, it wont do!" he said, as he stood thoughtful for a moment; "he might be for going down, after he has got the others down, to see if all is right; and if he should find I had let one off, he'd kill me as quick as he'd wink. No, no; I'll wait till he brings the others, and after he's gone, I'll let 'em all off, and find out what his game is. I dont like it; it's d—d suspicious; and I'll find out the bottom of it 'fore morning, and balk his deviltry."

Mike laid himself down again upon the settee, and remained silently puffing forth the smoke from his mouth for a short space of time, when a knock was heard at the outer door of the tap-room. He arose and unfastened it, and Wing and his comrades entered with the other six bound seamen. Fastening the door after they entered, Mike again led the way to the cellar-trap, in the passage-way. The Captain raised the trap cautiously, and found the steps clear, and the six bound seamen were thrust down into the cellar, as had been the others.

"Give me the lantern, Mike; I want to go down here, and see that there's no chance of a slip for these fellows."

Mike handed the lantern to Wing, who with Mardon descended into the cellar, and after a few moments returned. The trap was fastened down, and all went back to the tap-room.

"Now, Mike, we must have a drink all round," said Wing, as he placed the lantern upon the bar.

After they had swallowed the liquor, Wing ordered the four sailors back to the boat to wait for him and Mardon, who remained.

"Well, this job is safely over," said he, with evident satisfaction, as the four sailors left the tap-room.

"Not so safely over, neither," muttered Mike to himself, as he went to fasten the door.

"You must feed them fellows on bread and water, Mike, or anything you have a mind to, but that will keep them from starving. But I leave them in your care; if you let them starve, they will be no more trouble to me. But let's have some more whiskey, I am cursed dry." All three again drank. Wing and Mardon then turned from the bar, and went towards the door, as if to depart.

"But Captain, there's one part of the job that's not finished—the five hundred dollars you were to pay me," said Mike, as he stepped from behind the bar, in a voice as if he somewhat doubted the fulfilment of that most important part to him.

"Oh, the money," said Wing, in a dry, unconcerned manner. "O, that's all moonshine, Mike. You didn't suppose I was going to give you five hundred dollars? You must have taken me for a bigger fool than I am."

"You wont pay me the money, then?" said Mike, in an inquiring tone.

"I rather think not," answered the Captain, dryly.

"Then the bargain's broke, and I vow I'll let the fellows out," said Mike, quickly and with some spirit.

"But that would betray me, and you swore to keep the secret, Mike."

"And you agreed to pay me for't,' said Mike, with a growl.

"Well, that's a part of the bargain I can't fulfil, Mike," said Wing, with a careless laugh.

"If you don't, I swear I'll set the fellows free before morning," said Mike, in a tone that implied a determination to do as he said.

At this Wing approached him, and whispered in his ear words that produced an electrical effect upon Mike, who started back aghast, while he trembled in every joint. The perspiration oozed out from, and stood in beaded drops upon, his fat face. He stood a moment as if paralyzed, and then, in a voice that summoned up all his powers of speech, he exclaimed,

"In God's name, Will Wing! how came you to know this?"

"It matters not now for me to tell you; it is enough that I know it, Mike," said Wing, with a sarcastic smile upon his lips, as if pleased at the trepidation of the man before him. "But your secret is safe, if you keep mine; so good night. Remember, if you play me false, you shall pay dearly for it."

Wing passed his hand significantly across his throat, and up above his head, as he spoke, and with Mardon passed out from the tap-room, leaving Mike to ponder over the mysterious words which had produced such a startling effect upon him, and to recover from the state of surprise and trepidation he was in, as best he might.

The two hurried toward the pier where the boat lay in waiting, and in a short time they were alongside the brigantine.

"Well, Mardon, we are safe now, if there is none on board who will now betray us; and we can lay here as long as we wish in security," said Wing, as he touched the deck.

"I'll answer for them," said Mardon. "But the girl, what do you intend to do with her, Captain?"

"Blood and zounds! I had forgotten her!" said Wing, in a vehement tone, as if struck all aback. "She must not remain here, Mardon, that's certain. But what shall we do with her? I have it. Marshall must take care of her also. I'll go down and see how fares the grief-stricken beauty; we must take her ashore."

As he spoke, he made toward the companion-way, and descended into the cabin. It was dark as he entered, but soon the darkness was dispelled by a brilliant light, which shed a bright radiance around the small but splendid cabin, which was furnished in a style of oriental luxuriance.

Reclining upon a lounge, above which was a large and magnificent mirror, was a young female robed in white, who, as Wing entered and lighted up the cabin, rose up from her reclining posture, and sat with her elbow resting upon the arm of the lounge. She was a fair young creature, not exceeding eighteen years of age.

Her face was of that oval form so peculiarly lovely in woman. Her features were of the Grecian cast, and beautiful in the extreme, though now a saddened expression overspread them. Her large, dark eyes, shaded by extremely long, black, and curving lashes, were languid in expression; and their glance, when in a happier mood, must have been dangerously bewitching to all who encountered her gaze.

Her left hand was lost to the gaze in the rich tresses of her dark hair, which, parted above the middle of her fair, high brow, white as Parian marble, fell in luxuriant abundance to her neck and shoulders, whose whiteness rivalled the mountain snow. Her right hand, also, as if to hide its fair proportions from the eye, as it supported her head, was lost beneath the abundant ringlets which fell over it upon her rounded and beautifully-moulded arm in bewitching clusters, as if to protect that also from gaze.

The face of this fair young being was without the slightest color, pale as death. Its expression was deeply sorrowful, and indicated that some heart-stricken grief, anguish, and woe, were her's; and even now, as she gazed up to the man before her, a tear fell from each eye, glistening like pearl drops in the brilliant light of the cabin.

Wing stood for a moment gazing thoughtfully upon the beauteous but sorrowing female before him, and it seemed that a ray of pity was for an instant visible in the expression of his face, but the next he spoke in a tone that betokened his heart felt not what, for an instant, his face betrayed.

"Well, fair lady, you are ever weeping; is there no check to this grief? By the Lord! I should think the fountain of sorrow would ere long exhaust itself, at such free vent as you have given way to. But I have not come to talk of this, but to say that you cannot longer remain here; you must prepare for departure immediately."

"Where, O where would you take me?" asked the maiden, in a voice of apprehension, as she partly rose and then sank down again.

"Away from here, lady; where, it may be, no splendor like this around you may meet the eye, but where no harm shall come to you. So prepare, for your departure must be immediate."

"I am ready; but, O, I fear that harm is near—I fear harm from you; and why should I not? You have cruelly torn me from my home, my parents, friends, from everything that was dear to me on earth, and borne me I know not whither, far away from all. Have I no cause of fear from one who has done this? And have I no cause for the sorrow you make light of? In the name of Heaven, tell me, where are we? Where would you take me? Oh! do not let harm come to me!—swear, O swear it!"

"I have said, lady, no harm shall come to you."

"Will you swear it?"

"If you consider my oath a more sufficient guarantee of your safety, I will," said Wing, lightly, as if he considered but indifferently the oath he swore.

"Then if you mean me no harm, tell me, in heaven's name, what object you have in view with regard to me?"

"Why, to tell the truth, my fair griever, I have not concluded as to the ultimatum of the design I have in view," answered Wing, in a careless, indifferent manner.

The sorrowing maiden gazed for a moment im-ploringly into his face, while her dark eyes filled with tears, and then, in a voice of earnest supplication, at the same time sinking to her knees at his feet, said—

"O sir, why will you not restore me to my home—to my parents? Think, O think, of the many hearts you would cause by so doing to beat with the liveliest joy and unbounded happiness, that are now beating in the worst of misery at my cruel abduction, and are tortured in agonizing doubt at my unknown fate. Oh! take me back to my home; restore me to my parents, and I will bless you ever while I live, till my dying hour. You have, you must have some pity in your heart; in Heaven's name let it actuate you in my behalf."

The imploring attitude of the fair being, her agonized and beseeching looks, and tone of heart-rending supplication, would have melted the heart of any one to pity as it seemed. But it caused the heart of the unrelenting and unpitying man before whom she kneeled no emotion. He stood with a countenance unmoved, save that a smile played upon his lips, it seemed at the misery of the youthful suppliant at his feet.

In a light tone that assured of no sympathy for her sorrow, he spoke—

"No, no, my pretty one, I cannot take you back. I did not run the risk I did in securing the possession of your person, to be moved to pity by your words, or to restore you so soon to your home, from whence I took you. It would be mere boy's play to do this. No, no, you must not think of home; you must banish all thoughts of it, for you never again will return."

"Oh! say not so—say not I never again shall see my home, my parents; if you have a human heart, say not so."

A fresh outburst of overpowering grief choked the utterance of the fair captive, and burying her face in her hands, she wept aloud.

"Come, lady, I'm weary of this. Arise, for you must leave this place."

Wing uttered this in a quick, impatient tone, and moved as if to raise her from her kneeling posture. She started from him to her feet, and threw back the flowing tresses of her dark hair from her fearfully pallid face, and with her dark, Oriental eyes, suffused with tears fixed upon him, spoke in a tone calmer than before—

"If the misery you have caused those from whom you have torn me—if mine own agony will not move your callous heart to pity, and induce you to restore me to my home, take me back, and you shall have wealth beyond measure. My father is rich; he will load you with wealth if you will but restore me to his arms."

"Curses on your father!" said Wing, in a voice abrupt and malignant. "Did he possess the mines of Golconda, and would offer them as your ransom, I would reject his proffer. Nothing can or shall induce me to accede to your wish."

The maiden gazed with a look of wild alarm at the man before her, and in a voice of startling earnestness, exclaimed—

"Art thou a mortal, or a fiend ?"

"Either, as you wish," said Wing, in a light tone. "But I will have no more words ; here is your bonnet and shawl, you will need them to keep the night air from you. I will adjust them, with your permission."

"Will nothing induce you to return me ; will you not take me back ?" exclaimed the maiden, in a wild, agonizing voice, as she clasped her hands, and with a look of hopeless despair, gazed into the unmoved countenance of the wretch before her.

"Once and for all—no !" answered Wing, in a tone of determined resolve.

"Then I will die here now, rather than live longer in the power of such a fiend."

The maiden uttered these words in a high and spirited voice of fearful determination, and drawing back from the inhuman monster to whom she had in vain supplicated, drew from her bosom a small dagger, and with an arm nerved by despair, she forced the gleaming steel toward her breast.

Within a hair's breadth of its intended aim her arm was seized, and the dagger torn from her hand by Wing, who, utterly confounded at the sudden and unexpected attempt of the maiden to destroy her life, stood for a moment speechless, gazing at her. He held the dagger in his own hand, which would have gone unerringly to her heart, had he not so opportunely arrested the fatally aimed blow. At length he spoke—

"So, my pretty one, you would have met death by your own hand, had I not saved you. By the fiends ! you are too young, too beautiful to die. You shall live to thank me for the life I saved ere you die."

He placed his hand upon her shoulder as he spoke. She staggered at his touch, and with a piercing shriek that curdled the blood with horror in his veins, she fell lifeless to the floor. Wing raised the victim of his brutal inhumanity quickly up, and supporting her with one arm, he adjusted her bonnet to her head, and wrapping a large and magnificent shawl about her inanimate form, lifted her in his arms, after first imprinting a kiss upon her cold and marble-like brow, and disappeared from the cabin.

CHAPTER III.

WILL WING.

WE will now, with the reader's permission, go back some years prior to the events detailed in the two foregoing chapters, and bring up events, as they transpire in turn, to where we terminated in the second chapter.

Willard Wing, or Will, as he was always termed from boyhood, was the only child of a wealthy merchant of New York. He was the idol of his affectionate mother, who loved too blindly her dear little Will, as she always called him, for his own good in after life.

From the first, his every wayward whim, his every wish was gratified by his loving and too indulgent mother, who was often remonstrated with by her husband, who also tenderly loved his boy, but who saw the evil that would accrue from the too excessive indulgence of his wife.

But his arguments for the welfare of his son were always overcome by his wife, who, with little Will clasped in her arms, would always argue with the eloquence of love, that the indulgence she displayed toward him would never in the least prove detrimental to him in after years.

The father, a man of but few words, and easy in his disposition, would seldom contend long in argument with his wife, who invariably came off victor, and who always persuaded him that he was too fearful and over anxious about the welfare of his son.

Thus little Will, wholly under his mother's care, would always apply to her for any favor he wished, and rarely, if ever, was he denied. Thus he grew to the age of ten years, a petted, half-spoiled child. He was unusually clever for one of his years, so much so as to be remarked by every one who saw him. A handsome, rosy-cheeked little fellow, with a mischievous smile always upon his pouting lips, dark and roguishly expressive eyes, and his air in flowing ringlets—he was the favorite of all.

A large, noble, Newfoundland dog, a present from his father, was the constant companion of little Will, in the house or out. Whenever he roamed over the extensive grounds owned by his father, Carlo was ever by his side, and seemed to love his young master with a devotion rarely excelled by any of this species, which are ever affectionate. Will loved his noble dog as well in return—for he was once saved from drowning by the noble animal. Frolicking one day with Carlo around the borders of a pond, situated some distance in the rear of the house, he slipped down the steep bank into the water. His cries soon brought the faithful dog to his aid, who, at the moment his young master had fallen in, lay crouching upon the ground, with his head upon his fore paws, as if waiting for him to get some distance off and then to bound after him, as this had been the manner of their frolic. At the cries of distress, he sprang up, and bounded swiftly toward the pond, and plunging in, seized his young master by his clothes and swam with him to where the land sloped gently into the water. As the little fellow touched the shore, he ran off laughing, as if not in the least frightened at his immersion. Shaking the water from his shaggy coat, the noble dog bounded after him, and by his antics and gambolling, manifested the greatest joy at having rescued his young master from his late peril. From that hour the noble animal and young Will were equally favorites with all.

Beside his dog, Will had a pony also, a beautiful little animal, kind, docile, and gentle as a lamb; a present to him on his ninth birthday from his father. He soon learned to ride, and often would mount with the help of Carlo, who would stand by the side of the pony, while his master, first mounting his back, would thus easily seat himself in the saddle; and giving free rein to the gentle beast, would gallop gently along for several miles away from the house, followed by the faithful and well-trained Carlo. What with his pony and his dog, and having every indulgence, our little pet led a merry life, with nothing to mar his happiness till he reached his eleventh year, when he was deprived by death of his indulgent and affectionate mother; thus leaving him under the future care of his father, who being engaged in business pursuits, and most of his time and attention occupied thereby, could devote but a small share to the interest and advancement of his son. Thus Will grew to the age of fifteen, having since his mother's death followed the bent of his own inclinations, little or no more restraint being imposed upon him by his father than when before his mother's death. Whatever he wanted, he had; and if ever refused by his father, would manage, some way or other, to obtain what he desired.

He cared little or nothing for the commands of his father, who had now retired in opulence from all business pursuits, and now strove to correct the too free habits his son had contracted by over-indulgence and unrestraint. But he found this no easy task to execute; despite him, Will would have his own way and say, and do pretty much as he pleased. A quick, impetuous fellow, he would scarcely listen to any words of remonstrance from his father, and if he did, would give them not the slightest thought.

Finding all attempts to check the wayward and corrupt influences of his son, or to curb his imperious will, in vain, Mr. Wing determined to send him from home to an academy some distance away; where, by giving the preceptor instructions to be strict, or even severe with him, allowing only what would be absolutely necessary to his wants, he was in hopes to counteract the evil tendency of his son's nature acquired by former indulgence. He therefore informed Will of his intention, and told him to prepare immediately to depart from home. This determination on the part of his father did not suit Will, who till now had been surrounded by every luxury and comfort that wealth could bestow; and he openly and flatly refused to go.

"We will see, said his father, somewhat sternly. "I am determined to have my way, and be obeyed in this instance, my young blood; you shall go."

"But I wont, though," said Will, coolly, as he lay at length upon a lounge in his father's parlor, whipping his boot with his riding whip, and one hand patting the head of Carlo, his favorite.

Mr. Wing bit his lip with vexation at the reply of his son, but said no more upon the subject then. He left the house and was absent till the next day, when he returned, and told his son that he had been to the academy, and that he must be prepared to accompany him there the next morning. Will saw his father was determined, and he left him without a reply.

At the hour set the next morning for the departure, Will was nowhere to be found. A search was commenced for him about the house and around the grounds, but his whereabouts could not be discovered. The day passed and he did not return. A week, a month passed, and he was still an absentee. Month after month till three years had fled, and Willard Wing was not heard from. Mr. Wing was distressed at his son's unknown whereabouts and absence, and often said he would give half his wealth to have him return. As he sat one morning in his library, engaged in looking over the contents of a daily journal, he was interrupted by the entrance of some person, who with an unbecoming familiarity accosted him with—

"How are you, old gent. ?"

Mr. Wing raised his eyes to the intruder, and, beheld a neatly clad, handsome young sailor enter, and with a rolling gait advance toward him. He gazed with unbounded surprise at the unannounced and unexpected visitor, who now, seated in a chair, with his feet upon another, was smoking a fragrant cigar with the greatest composure, and with the air of impudent familiarity.

"You have the advantage of me, my young tar," said Mr. Wing, in a pleasant tone, as he laid the paper upon the table before him and rose up.

",The young scrape-grace is perfectly at home here —he takes it very coolly!" he muttered to himself, as he rose from his seat.

"Perfectly at home, as you see, old gent," said the young sailor, in a saucy tone, who had overheard the words of Mr. Wing.

As he spoke he took off his shining tarpaulin and exclaimed, with a laugh—

"Why, dad, don't you know me?"

Mr. Wing sprang toward him, exclaiming eagerly, in a joyful voice—

"Willard, my son, is it indeed you? Thank Heaven, you have returned!"

The young sailor was indeed his son. He warmly embraced the long absented youth, and seemed overjoyed at his return. He eagerly questioned him as to where he had been during his long absence, and pressed him to relate all that had happened to him since he left home.

"Well, dad, I will tell you all about it; sit down," said Will, tossing the half burnt cigar out of the window; and after his father was seated, began: "You remember the morning you were to take me to the academy, don't you, dad? ha—ha—"

The young sailor laughed heartily as he asked this question, and his father smiled also.

"I slipped cable and went to sea that morning. I left the house before daylight, determined not to go to the academy, and went down to the wharves among the shipping, resolving to go to sea. After wandering around for three hours, I found a ship that was to sail that day for Calcutta. I stole aboard of her unobserved, and stowed myself out of sight under some old sails and rigging upon deck, and laid there till nearly night, when of a sudden I felt my ankle clutched by the hand of some person, who bellowed out in astonishment, 'What the devil have we got here?' I was snaked out rather unceremoniously from my hiding place, and the whole ship's company stared at me with greedy eyes and gaping mouths.

"'How the devil came you aboard here?' asked one of the sailors, a stout built, surly looking chap, who shook me in a rough manner. 'Do you know we are out to sea?' asked the same fellow, again giving me another shake.

"'I suppose we are, if you say so,' said I, looking around over the blue ocean, and seeing no land in view. The ship had every sail spread and was ploughing gallantly along through the blue waves and leaving a foaming track behind. The scene was a novel and exciting one to me, and I capered about the deck like one half mad, much to the amusement of the crew. The Captain asked what I had come aboard the ship for, and I told him I wanted to go to sea. He told me he believed I was a run-away young rascal, and threatened to throw me overboard. But he altered his mind, I believe, and told me I should go to sea if I wished. Before the next morning I experienced symptoms of sea-sickness, and for two days suffered intolerably; and heartily wished I had gone to the academy. But repentance came too late.

"After a long and tedious passage, during which I suffered every hardship from the crew, being kicked and knocked about, and bruised from head to heel, the ship arrived at her destined port. A week afterwards I got aboard of a British ship, bound to Liverpool.

"We had been ten days out from Calcutta, when we were chased, overhauled, and captured by a piratical schooner. The pirates robbed the ship of every thing of any value that could be stowed away in the schooner, and then fired the ship, leaving the crew to save themselves the best way they could. The pirate chief took me aboard the schooner, and seemed to have taken a great fancy to me. He dressed me like his men, buckled a black belt around me, and stuck in a brace of pistols. Thus accoutred, and in high favor with the pirate chief, who treated me with the greatest kindness, I lived quite a free and easy life for upwards of a year, in the schooner, which during that time captured a number of prizes. One day, during a severe fight with a large and well armed Indiaman, a sail was discovered bearing down upon them. The stranger was soon made out to be a sloop of war under English colors, bearing directly for them, and rapidly nearing.

"The pirates retreated to the deck of the schooner and hauled off from the Indiaman, leaving a score of their number, with the chief, dead upon the deck. I remained, and was twice shot at by two of the pirates, as they left the Indiaman, because I would not follow. The schooner was captured within sight of us, being so crippled by the guns of the Indiaman that she was unable to escape from the sloop of war, which was a fast sailer, and soon overhauled and captured her.

"After clearing the deck of the slain pirates, and repairing what damage had been sustained during the conflict, the Indiaman was again soon upon her course, bound for Liverpool, where without further interruption she arrived. After a stay of two months in that port I went to London, and after a considerable stop in that metropolis, I shipped for the West Indies. After a short stay in Havana, I took passage in a brig bound for Boston, from which place I arrived here last night, and here I am."

Mr. Wing listened eagerly to the narrative of his son, and was much rejoiced at his safe return.

"But what do you now intend to do, my son?" asked he, as Will ended.

"Live at home like a gentleman, as long as this lasts, and then if you are not disposed to fork over liberally, why, I'm off to sea again," answered Will, as he pulled forth from his pockets two bags, and emptied a glittering pile of sovereigns, upon the floor at his feet.

"From the looks of this I should judge you would not make a demand very soon upon me," said Mr. Wing, with a smile, as he gazed at the heap of gold. "But how did you acquire this, my son?"

"Oh, I supplied myself when I left the pirate schooner," said Will, carelessly gathering up the gold. "This and as much more I took from the private treasury of the pirate chief, during the battle with the Indiaman, after I found the pirate was getting the worst of it. This will last me some time, with moderate living, after which I must depend upon you for a supply, dad, or I am off," said Will, pocketing the gold.

Mr. Wing sighed, and gazed at his thoughtless and self-abandoned boy, with a look of deep commiseration. A tear fell from his eye, and grasping his hand, he said in a tone of deep feeling—

"O my son! my son! I fear for you! I fear the reckless turn of your disposition will be your downfall —your ruin. My son, discard from your mind all such reckless and abandoned thoughts as by your utterance betray their existence. Oh! turn not away; for the love I bear you, for the cherished hopes I have of you, listen to my words—words that come from my very heart, and meant for your good. Let not your tongue give utterance to such ignoble thoughts; but let higher, nobler thoughts take place of those which have so estranged you from the path of rectitude, and which, if you foster them, will be your bane. By the memory of your fond mother, I pray you, my son, give heed to my words in time to profit by them, as you surely will if you conform to their advice. Oh! remain here, live with me—and I should wish you to live, my son, a true gentleman; but not a profligate, as you, if left to the guidance of the corrupt impulses of your heart, would live. I have wealth; you shall share with me in all that wealth conduces to the happiness of mortals."

The earnest appeal of the father was here interrupted by his obdurate son, who, in an unfeeling tone, said, as he withdrew his hand from the grasp of his sire—

"Come, father, no more preaching; I will not hear it. I did not come here to be lectured about my morals, nor will I be. I had enough of these lessons of morality before I went away. I came here to live, while my money holds out, and live I will, to my own liking; so no more preaching. After some years have passed over my head, I may perhaps settle down in a more staid manner of living, like yourself; but if there is any enjoyment to be taken in this world, I will have my share now while I am young. Your words will not effect any change in the profligate, as you choose to term me, father of mine; so you may save the utterance of any more advice."

The handsome, but perverted youth, spoke in a light tone, that showed his father's words had not made the least impression upon his mind; and that he mocked at all affection entertained for his grieving sire, whose life he was embittering by the loose and reckless principles, which, young as he was, had become instilled deeply in his heart, and to which he freely abandoned himself.

Six months passed away, and Willard Wing, by a course of profligacy hardly conceivable in one so young, had expended the last sovereign of the thousand he had brought home.

One evening, as Mr. Wing sat in his library, his favorite place of resort, his mind dwelling painfully upon the course of life pursued by his son, he was startled by the abrupt entrance of the young spendthrift himself, who in a more abrupt manner made a demand upon his father for a thousand dollars.

Mr. Wing gazed with surprise and pity at his son, who had thrown himself carelessly upon a chair, his fingers playing with a magnificent gold chain which he wore around his neck, and his eyes fixed with a dreamy stare upon the carpet, while he hummed partial snatches of a song in a light tune. After a moment's thoughtful gaze at his son, Mr. Wing spoke—

"Your demand is great and unexpected, my son. A thousand dollars! Can it be possible that your extravagance has been so lavish as to have swallowed up all the money you returned with? Can it be possible that you have in six months made away with nearly five thousand dollars? Speak, my son, is that all gone?"

"Every farthing!" was the laconic and unconcerned reply of the young prodigal, continuing to hum as before.

"All gone!" said his father, in an abstracted tone of surprise, as he rose and paced the room in a thoughtful mood for a moment.

"Yes, all gone, father—not a rap left!" said the young spendthrift again, in a light, careless tone. "I must have some more, father, or I must dispose of my horses and all else that I have, to pay a debt which, if not paid to-morrow, why I shall have to go to prison, that is all; at least, so swears my indulgent and obliging creditor."

"How much is the debt?" asked Mr. Wing.

"A little short of a thousand," answered Will.

"Quite a modest little sum for a youngster like yourself to owe. But send your creditor to me, and I will pay the debt," said Mr. Wing, as he sat himself down again.

"He's got me now. No, that won't do," said Will to himself, as his father sat down with his back toward him. "But I told him to come to you, father; but he swore he would not go a step after it."

"Then I will go to him," said Mr. Wing, in a very obliging tone.

"Oh! the devil! you are too willing," said the son to himself, as if not particularly well pleased at the offer of his father. "But, father, I wish to pay the debt to-night—in fact, I promised it."

"You promised, eh? Well, I suppose you would not break your word for any consideration," said Mr. Wing, in a sarcastic tone.

"Not in this case," said Will, with a yawn, as he spoke.

"Well, you shall keep your promise," said his

HOISTING THE PIRATES' FLAG.

father, rising from his seat, and going to a secretary which stood at the side of the room opposite the entrance. After a moment or two he turned to his son, and said: "Willard, here is a five hundred dollar bank note; you can satisfy your creditor with this for to-night; to-morrow you shall have the balance."

Will rose, and advancing toward his father, took the proffered note, and thrust it carelessly into his vest pocket.

"I can do with this to-night, I suppose," said he, as he walked out of the room, without a word of thanks for the money he had received.

He instantly left the house and proceeded to the ferry, for the purpose of crossing to the city, for his father's residence was in Brooklyn. Half an hour from the time he left the house, and he stood at the door of one of the most notorious gambling saloons of the city. He entered from the street into a spacious and elegantly furnished drinking saloon, which was thronged with young and middle aged men, who were regarded fashionables of the day. Six young men were kept busily engaged behind the bar, dealing out liquor to the numerous patrons of the establishment; and the ringing of tumblers upon the marble slab was constant. Passing along through this thronged saloon toward a stairway, Will ascended to a gorgeously furnished billiard-room above. It was brilliantly lighted, and contained a numerous company. The walls of this apartment were hung with costly and beautiful paintings of every description. The ceiling was painted in fresco, in a high style of art, and elicited the admiration of every new beholder. A costly carpet of the highest and richest colors covered the floor, and around the apartment were a number of lounges of the costliest pattern, for the convenience and accommodation of the frequenters of the room. This splendid room contained a dozen billiard tables, besides roulette, card, and other tables for gambling purposes. Around one of the former was gathered quite a throng to witness a trial game between two noted and experienced players.

As young Wing entered he immediately proceeded towards this table. As he reached it he was accosted by a fashionably dressed young man, who grasped and shook his hand quite heartily, and said in a tone of some little surprise—

"Ah, Will, you here again?"

"I thought you were done up to the last dollar, last night."

"So I was, Ned," rejoined Wing.

"So you have come to look on, eh? I did not expect to see you here again so soon. Made a raise, eh?"

"Of a small sum," said Wing, as he pulled forth the five hundred dollar note given him by his father and held it to the view of his companion.

"Five hundred! Quite a show. But don't, for God's sake! lose it all to-night, Will. How did you get so much out of the old man?"

"Easy enough," answered Will, laughing. "I humbugged the old fellow, by telling him a cock-and-bull story about a debt I had got to pay, or go to prison. He could not bear the thoughts of his son being immured in the walls of a prison, so forked over five hundred to-night, and to-morrow he gives me as much more. But I must get this broke; I want gold for it."

"Old Jewhard will give you gold, at the roulette-table, Will," said his comrade, taking his arm.

Both walked up to the table, and Will, tossing the bank note towards a man who sat behind the table, said,—

"I want gold for that."

The man snatched up the note, and examined it minutely through a pair of green spectacles, and then smoothed it out upon the table before him.

"I'll accommodate you for a half eagle," he said, with a glance at Will.

"Do it. You are very reasonable," said Will, with a sarcastic smile.

The keeper of the roulette-table counted out the gold—four hundred and ninety-five dollars, in whole and half eagles, reserving one half eagle for the accommodation.

Wing, counting it over after him, soon transferred it to his pockets. As he was turning to leave, a young man stepped up to the table and placed an eagle upon a small red square, one of a number which environed the roulette-table.

"Do you set double O red?" inquired the banker now setting the wheel in rapid motion.

"Yes," answered the young man, tremblingly.

The banker dropped a small ivory ball into the revolving wheel, and the young man who had staked the eagle watched with eager eye the rapid revolutions of the wheel and ball. Both at length stopped.

"You have won," said the banker, as he counted out thirty-two eagles, and pushed them across the table to the lucky winner.

The young man had won thirty-two times the amount he had staked. A slight smile played upon his lips—his eye brightened as he took up the gold he had won. Counting out ten eagles, he placed them upon double O red again.

"You will not win on that again," said Ned, the companion of Wing.

"I will try my luck, at any rate," said the young man, in return.

"Black wins," said the banker a moment after, as he drew the ten eagles toward him.

"I knew you would lose," said Ned with a sneer, as if at the folly of the latter.

"That's my business," said the other sharply, in reply; and he placed upon double O red ten eagles more.

"Black wins," said the banker again, as the ball and wheel stopped, and with a small rake he pulled the money towards him.

"I'll bet on O O black this time," said the young man, as he placed upon that color ten eagles again.

"Red wins," drawled out the banker, as he drew the third stakes toward him.

The loser said not a word, but placed three eagles quietly upon single O red.

"Red wins," said the banker, as he pushed six eagles to the winner, who immediately staked them again upon single O red.

"Black wins," said the banker, and he drew the money toward the pile of gold before him. With a curse at his ill-luck, the young man left the table, and the room.

"The fool ought to have gone when he won the first time," said Ned, as if half angry at the manner in which the young man had staked his bets.

"But come, Wing, let's play a game at billiards."

"Not now, Ned. I have a mind to try my luck once more here; I have always lost as yet, but luck may turn. Here goes an eagle; if I lose it, I'll forswear the roulette-table."

Wing placed an eagle upon single O black, and won. The banker tossed him two eagles; he had won double the amount he had staked.

"I'll stake the three on black again," said Wing, as he placed them as before.

"I will bet on the red," said his companion, staking an eagle.

"I bet on the red," said a new comer, at that moment stepping up to the table, and laying five eagles upon red.

"All set!" said the banker, setting the wheel in motion, the next moment dropping in the little ivory ball. "Black wins," he drawled out, and Wing took up the six eagles which had been staked upon red, and again staked the nine upon black.

His friend, Ned Harding, and the other, bet each an eagle upon red.

"Black wins," said the banker, tossing Wing sixteen eagles, which he, with the two that had been staked by the others, again staked upon black.

Harding and the other again bet upon red, each staking five eagles, confident that black would not again win.

CHAPTER IV.

THE GAMBLER.

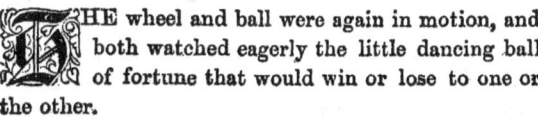HE wheel and ball were again in motion, and both watched eagerly the little dancing ball of fortune that would win or lose to one or the other.

"Black wins," said the banker, pushing across the table to Wing three hundred and sixty dollars in gold, and raking toward him the ten eagles staked by the other.

Wing staked the whole of this against black.

"You are a fool, Will, you cannot win the fifth time," said Ned Harding, placing one hundred dollars upon red. The same amount was staked by the other on the same color.

"All set?" said the banker, who in a moment again set the wheel in rapid motion; and again the little ball was dancing around within it.

Harding cast a glance at Will; and said emphatically, "You will lose this time." Will smiled, but said nothing; his smile expressed indifference and unconcern.

"Black wins," said the banker in his usual calm tone. He pulled toward him the two hundred dollars bet upon the red color, and counting out seven hundred and twenty dollars pushed that amount across to Wing.

Harding and the other young man uttered each an oath of surprise, at the unusual good fortune of Wing, and their faces betrayed angry disappointment.

Wing laughed, and counting out one thousand dollars from the pile before him, was about to place it upon the color that had proved so lucky to him, when his hand was stayed by Hardinge, who said in an impressive manner—

"For God's sake, Will, don't stake that amount again upon black; you will lose it. You have won five times in succession upon that color; you cannot win the sixth, it is impossible. Come, let's leave the table." He took the arm of Wing as he spoke, and tried to persuade him to leave; but in vain. Hard, indeed, is it to entice the gambler, when fortune favors him, from the exciting game. One, two, five thousand is not enough, if there is yet more to be won. He will not leave till he has swept the board or lost his all.

"No, Harding, I shall not go," said Wing, disengaging his arm from that of his friend. "I have lost at that table four times the amount I have won to-night. I will have it back, or leave this thousand there also. I have always had ill luck here; it has turned to-night, and I will make the most of it. It is not impossible for me to be winner the sixth time; at any rate I will risk it. I will stake a thousand upon black," he said, as he turned to the table and laid the money where he had five times before staked his bets, and as many times won.

"If it is not impossible, it is improbable that you will win again, Wing; you but tempt your luck to bet again," said Harding, in a tone that expressed not the least doubt but that his friend would lose. I have but ten dollars left, and shall stake it upon red," said he, placing an eagle upon that color.

"And I bet one hundred dollars upon red," said the other player, as he staked that amount.

The wheel and ball were again in motion, and Wing, considerably excited, watched them with the deepest interest. A few seconds and the banker, muttering an oath, drawled out—"Black wins."

Wing clutched up the thousand dollars he had staked, and in a moment two thousand more were pushed over to him by the banker.

A number had now collected around the roulette table, and every eye was fixed upon young Wing, who, as he gathered up the two thousand dollars and counted it over, placed it upon the black color with a calm indifference that surprised the by-standers.

"How many times has he won?" asked a man of another, as he stepped up to the table.

"Six times on black," was the answer.

"What does he bet this time?"

"Two thousand dollars."

"He's a fool. I bet one thousand dollars upon red," said the man, who was a noted gambler, and reputed wealthy.

"And I the same," said another individual, placing two five hundred dollar notes upon the red color.

"All set!" said the banker, after a moment's pause.

Again the wheel of fortune was in motion, and its horizontal revolutions seemed more rapid than ever before. All eyes were rivetted upon the ivory ball that danced about within the wheel as if possessed by magic. The silence around the table was in a moment broken by sudden exclamations of surprise, that burst from all who were gathered there.

Wing was the seventh time a winner. He took up the two thousand dollars he had staked, and in a moment received four thousand more from the banker.

All were amazed at the unusual and extraordinary success of the young gambler, who, flushed with success, and confident of still more, said in a voice of high excitement, "I will bet the four thousand dollars upon black," and he threw down the money upon the table, with a reckless air of confidence.

"Its folly!" its folly!" exclaimed a dozen voices at once.

"I will not take the bet," said the banker. "Eight thousand dollars would break me, should you again win."

"As you please," said Wing, taking up the money, and placing the two thousand he held in his hand with it, he coolly thrust the bank notes into his pocket

and walked away from the table the winner of upwards of seven thousand dollars.

"Well, Ned, that was not bad, though, was it?" said Wing, in an elated tone, as he took the arm of his friend, with whom he walked slowly from the roulette table. "Seven thousand dollars! gods! my luck turned to-night with a vengeance. I have won back all the money I ever lost there, with compound interest. "I'll live a merry life while this lasts. But how much did you lose, Ned?"

"All I had—one hundred and eighty dollars," answered Ned, in a tone of vexation.

"Well, here, take this!" said Wing, as he drew from his pocket the roll of money, and pulling out a hundred dollar note, handed it to Harding, who refused it. "Not a word, Ned; take it," said Wing, as he placed the note in his hand. "Now, Ned, for a game at billiards!" said he, as he forced the note upon his friend, and turned towards a billiard table. "I shall relish a game much now, come!"

As he spoke, he felt the gripe of a hand upon his arm, and turning round he beheld, to his utter amazement, his father.

The winning of seven thousand dollars, or the loss of ten times that amount, would not have produced the effect upon him, as did the sight of his father before him.

He stood as if paralysed before the gaze of his father, and uttered not a word. The wildest amazement was depicted upon his face, as he stood dumb with astonishment at the unexpected appearance of his father, who gazed at him with looks that bespoke equal astonishment and bitter sorrow.

"Is this indeed you, my son—here in this place?" he said, with deep emotion. "O God! that I have lived to see you—my son—a gambler!" The father uttered this in a voice of intense feeling and deepest agony; and remained silent, as if overpowered by his feelings, and his face, by its expression, told how great was the shock he had received at the discovery he had made respecting his son. He mastered his feelings after a moment, and spoke in a quick and energetic tone of authority—

"Willard, you must return that money!"

"But I wont, though," said the young man, who had now somewhat recovered his usual recklessness of character; and, with a laugh, he turned as if to leave his father, saying, "You must think I am a fool, to return the money I have won fairly."

He uttered this in a scoffing tone of voice, as he turned upon his heel.

"Willard, stay," said his father, peremptorily. "Return that money from whence you received it; and leave this cursed place instantly, or from this moment call yourself no son of mine," said the father, in a severe tone. "Do it, or I disown and disinherit you."

The young gambler hesitated, he had not expected

this; a severe struggle was going on within him.

To give up and relinquish the large amount of money he had just won so easily, was to him a difficult and extremely severe thing to do.

The thoughts of parting with the seven thousand dollars seemed to cut him to the very soul, and he stood motionless, as one without life.

"You hesitate, my son. I will no more command," said his father, breaking silence. "As you think best, so you may do. Return the money you have so basely obtained; or keep it and purchase your disinheritance; either, at your option. I stay but a moment longer in this cursed place to know your decision."

The young man hesitated now but an instant; the thought of being disinherited, as he knew by the stern, determined manner of his father he should be, at length overcame the reluctance to part with his heavy winnings. He took forth the money, and handing it to his father, said—

"Here it is; but I will not return it."

"Is here the whole amount you won?" asked his father, as he took the roll of bank notes.

"Yes," answered Will.

"I will return it, then, if here is all. Do not deceive me. If you go home with one dollar that comes from this gambling hell, I own you no son of mine."

"You have the whole!" said Will, in no very pleasing tone. His father turned, and approached the roulette table.

"I've saved a thousand, and he'll be none the wiser for it," said Will to his friend, who had heard what had passed between the father and son. "This is aggravating," he muttered; "to win seven thousand dollars, and then be compelled to give it up. In the name of all the fiends, how came he here!" exclaimed the young man, in a low tone of fearful passion. "Curse him! he followed me from home. Were it not that one day I hope to be heir to all his wealth, I would—but I will not say."

The young gambler, wickedly cursing his father, now left the gaming saloon.

It was ten o'clock that evening when Mr. Wing returned to his residence, with a heart full of sorrow and agony, caused by his son's profligate career. The worst of all vices he had himself discovered that his son was guilty of—gambling.

As Will had said, his father followed him to the gaming house, entered after him, and discovered himself in the manner we have related.

It was near midnight when young Will left the drinking saloon half intoxicated, for the ferry, which he reached but in time for the last passage.

After leaving the boat on the other side of the ferry, he staggered along towards home, and had nearly reached it, when he received a blow upon his head, from some one behind, which felled him insensible to the earth.

"You've killed him, Ned!" said a low, deep voice, as the young man fell to the ground.

"No I haven't—he's only stunned," said another voice, that of Ned Harding. "I could curse his father as heartily as he did himself. But for him, we might have had a richer prize. But as it is, he's got over fifteen hundred about him—I'll ease him of that! There, I've got all. Now let's take him to his house, and leave him at the door. I do not wish he should die here, as perhaps he may. By the Lord! his face is cold; come, help me quickly to bear him to the house, it's but a few steps."

The two robbers lifted the inanimate form of Wing, and hurriedly bore him to his house, where, setting him against the door, they gave a loud knock and fled.

Mr. Wing, who had not yet retired, but sat in agony of feeling, waiting his son's return, was roused by the loud knock at the door, and instantly went thither. As he opened the door, the body of his son, which had been set upright against it, fell in upon the floor.

A cry of horror burst from the father as he beheld his son, who lay as if dead, at his feet.

He alarmed the servants of the house, who were soon upon the spot, and the insensible young man was taken from the doorway to the apartment nearest at hand.

It was found that life had not fled, and a physician was instantly sent for. The young man had received a severe wound upon the back of his head, which bled profusely.

"He has been knocked down, robbed, and nearly murdered," said Mr. Wing, upon examining the person of his son. "Oh! may this be a lesson to him, such as he will ever remember!" said he, with deepest emotion, as he gazed on his half murdered son.

Two weeks from that night—Will having perfectly recovered from the effects of the wound he had received—one fair morn he was about to depart from his father's house for the University at Cambridge. His father wished him to go there, and strenuously urged him, during the time he had been confined to the house, to consent to his wishes. The young man at length yielded to his earnest solicitations, and consented to enter the University, to the great joy of his father, who fancied that he perceived signs of reform in the morals of his son.

That his son might abandon the profligate mode of life he had hitherto led, and for the future lead an altered and better life, was the sincere prayer of Mr. Wing, who yet loved his boy, despite his faults.

Will had solemnly sworn never to enter a gambling house, or to indulge more the passion for gaming, that had, young as he was, became so deeply instilled into his soul. With his father's blessing, and prayer for his future welfare, the young man departed from home.

Three months passed away, and Mr. Wing had received no word from him, when one day a letter came to him, which, by the post-mark, he knew to be from his son. He hailed with delight the welcome messenger from his absent boy, and hastily tore it open. The epistle read as follows:—

"Harvard University, Cambridge.

"DEAR FATHER,—You will forgive me for not writing you before this time, for not doing which I can offer no sufficient reason. I arrived here safely, and am very much pleased and contented. I have passed three months here very pleasantly, and I hope profitably. The students here are a fine set of young men, and I like their society much better than that of my former associates. There is one young man here to whom I am particularly attached. I became acquainted with him shortly after my arrival, and we very soon become friends. He is of a poor family, but a noble fellow. I learned his history, and became deeply interested in him. He had nearly completed his studies when I came here; but shortly after my arrival he received a death-blow to all his hopes, by a letter from his father, stating that he could no longer keep him there, as poverty deprived him of the means of so doing. The young fellow was absolutely bowed down with grief at this news; and the thoughts of being obliged to leave, when he had so nearly completed his studies, rendered him perfectly disconsolate. He was in arrears, and this troubled him the most. Unknown to him, I paid them, and offered him money from my fund. He refused it. I forced it upon him as a loan, in order to enable him to stay. I have continued since to supply his wants, for I love him as a brother. By so doing, and by the expenses I have myself incurred, I have exhausted my funds to the last dollar. A remittance would be most thankfully and gratefully received, by your son,

"WILLARD WING."

"Noble, generous boy!" exclaimed Mr. Wing, as he finished the perusal of his son's letter, in a voice of rapturous delight. "Thank God! he is saved from the abyss of ruin that threatened inevitably his downfall, as I feared. May Heaven grant he has seen the error of his former ways, and for the future walk in the path of honor and rectitude!"

With this the kind father folded the letter, and instantly prepared to write to his son. The letter completed, he inclosed a remittance of five hundred dollars, and ere an hour after he had received his son's letter, his was on its way back.

Two months passed, and Mr. Wing received another letter from his son. It was brief, and as follows:—

"MY DEAR FATHER,—I am again under the necessity of requesting another remittance, as I have very nearly expended the five hundred you sent me.
"Yours,   "WILLARD WING."

Not a word escaped the lips of Mr. Wing as he read that letter; and forthwith forwarded the desired remittance to his son.

Hardly had a month passed, when he received another demand for money from his son; and for a year after his demands were frequent, and supplied by his father as often as made; till one day came a letter, stating that he wanted and must have two thousand dollars. To this Mr. Wing wrote back a decided refusal. He had already remitted more than would have supported three young men handsomely; and, for the first time, he refused his demand. He had for some time mistrusted and doubted the truth of what his son had represented to him in his several letters, and feared that most of the money he had sent him was squandered away, or worse, lost at the gaming-table.

A week from the day he sent the letter refusing the last demand, the young man made his appearance at home, having been absent a year and five months. The meeting between the father and son was not very cordial; neither expressing any very great joy at seeing the other.

One evening about a month afterward Willard entered the billiard-room for the first time since his return—his former place of resort. The first person he encountered there was his former associate, Ned Harding.

After cordially greeting each other—Will little suspecting that he whom he so heartily greeted was the one who had waylaid and robbed him a year and a half before—Ned said to him,—

"Wing, this is the last time you will see me here; to-morrow I'm off."

"So you have repented of your ways, and are going to reform," said Wing, laughing.

"The reform I think of making is in my purse, which has been most shockingly low of late," said Ned, in return. "I am going to engage in a more profitable business than playing has ever proved to me."

"What is that?" asked Wing.

"Step back here, Will, and I will tell you."

The two seated themselves upon a lounge, beyond the hearing of any one in the hall.

"Now, Ned, what is this business? I have a great curiosity to know," said Wing, in a low tone.

"Promise secrecy, Will, before I tell you."

"I promise."

"Well, then; I have shipped in a vessel that before sunrise sails from here, bound to the coast of Africa, for slaves."

"Shipped in a slaver!" exclaimed Wing, in a tone of surprise.

"Hush! not so loud; Will, I do not care to have it known by every one. You seem surprised."

"I am, Ned. You shipped for a slaving voyage! I have a mind to ship myself. I will, if there is a chance," he said, in a tone of sudden determination, "Who, and where is the captain of this slaver?"

"He is here, in this room. If you wish, I will introduce you."

"Do so, Ned."

The two young men arose from the lounge, and approached a tall, powerfully-built, dark-looking man at the other end of the room, who was standing by himself, smoking a cigar, and watching two players engaged at a game of billiards.

"I should take him for one engaged in some such business," said Wing, in a low tone, as they neared this individual. "He is not sparing in point of dress. What a massive gold chain he wears!"

"He lives like a gentleman on shore," said Ned, "has plenty of gold, and spends it freely. He has made three successful voyages, and enriched himself."

"What has he come here for?" asked Wing.

"That is a part of his business I know nothing of," answered Harding, as he caught the eye of the slaver captain, and addressing him, introduced Wing. The three, stepping aloof from all others, were in a moment engaged in close conversation.

CHAPTER V.

THE SEA SWALLOW.

THE next morning at sunrise a topsail schooner, of about one hundred and fifty tons, sailed from New York bay, with her lower canvass spread to a fine breeze, that impelled her over the blue waves of the Atlantic at a goodly speed. She was a fine looking craft, and her build betokened that the speed of the wind was hers.

The deck of the schooner was covered with loose hay, and only three or four coarsely clad seamen were visible about the craft.

She held on her course over the broad blue Atlantic, till the land faded from the sight, and nothing but the blue ocean was visible to the eye.

At length appeared upon her deck another individual, a tall and powerfully built seaman, who with a glass scanned the horizon around for a moment, and then in a voice loud and heavy, hailed—

"On deck, all hands."

In a moment, upward of fourscore seamen made their appearance at this call; among them were Wing and Harding.

"Clear the deck of this hay, we have no longer need of its disguise," said the Captain of the craft, who was the same individual whom we noticed at the billiard room, as the slaver Captain, the night before.

The crew fell to work in obedience to the command of the Captain, and the deck was soon cleared of the hay that covered it. After this being accomplished the Captain spoke to the crew in this wise.

"My men, a few of you are deceived in reference to the character of this craft. She is no slaver, nor ever has been, neither have I ever been engaged in that traffic. Under this flag she has sailed, and now sails, and will till she lies beneath the blue waves she has so gallantly rode for years."

As the Captain spoke he unrolled a square of black bunting that he held in his hand, at the sight of which a murmur of surprise came from a part of the crew.

"A few of you shipped to go on a slaving voyage; the others were aware that slave stealing was not the character of the schooner. Which is the worse, I ask you, to sail the whole wide waters of this globe under a free commission, taking no life; or sail from the African coast loaded with human beings, doomed to perpetual slavery, worse than death? Any of you who would engage in this pursuit, I have no fears will object to sail under my flag—a free one. But if there is any among you who would not sail with me, he can depart." And as the Captain spoke, he ordered a boat to be towed alongside. "All who would go, are free to depart in that boat," said he, as the boat lay alongside.

Young Harding made his way to the vessel's side and leaped into it, casting a glance towards Wing, as if expecting he would follow.

But in this he was disappointed. Wing laughed, and bestowed upon him a slurring epithet.

No other followed Harding, who remained alone in the boat for some moments, when the Captain asked if there were any more who would go.

No answer was returned, and the Captain said to Harding, "You go alone; cast off."

"Hold, I will not be the only one to go," said Harding, as he sprang out of the boat, just as it was going to be cast off from the schooner.

"If you go, Wing, I go also," said he, as he gained the deck.

"I go sure," said Wing. "I served an apprenticeship in a piratical schooner, and am used to the business. Of the two evils, buccaneering or slaving, if I where to choose the least, it would be the former

You would steal a load of Africans and sell them into slavery, but have scruples about robbing a vessel! A conscientious young fellow, truly!" Wing spoke this in an ironical tone, and a sneering expression rested upon his face.

Harding bit his lip, but returned no reply.

"Open the hatches, and up with the guns, my lads," was the order that at this moment came from the Captain.

The hatches were opened, and preparations made for hoisting the guns of the schooner, which were in the hold below, and in less than an hour, ten guns were ranged upon the deck, five on a side.

Hardly had this arrangement been completed, when a sail was reported from the look-out.

"Where away?" hailed the Captain.

"Three points on our weather quarter," answered the look-out.

The captain sprang into the main rigging, and levelled a glass in the direction the sail had been discovered. He examined the distant sail through his glass attentively for a short time, when, as if apparently satisfied with the scrutiny, he descended from the rigging to the deck.

"That fellow is a cutter from New York harbor," said the captain to the first officer. "We passed him this morning, and he is now in full chase after us."

"He'll have his trouble for his pains," remarked the officer, in a tone of confidence. "Is it possible the schooner has been suspected?" he remarked to the captain, in a tone of inquiry.

"Yes; I saw a fellow this morning who knows me and the schooner," rejoined the captain. "He has given information, and that fellow on our quarter is a cutter in chase of us. Let him come up within a mile, Mr. Covell, and then loose the topsails. It must be the devil's craft that will then overhaul the 'Sea Swallow.'"

Uttering this in a voice of pride, that bespoke confidence in the speed of his vessel, the captain went below to the cabin.

The cutter, under full sail, gained rapidly upon the pirate craft, and soon was within the distance named by the captain—one mile, when the deep boom of a gun was heard.

"Aloft there, lads, and shake out the topsails, lively," was the order from the officer of the "Sea Swallow," as the gun was fired from the cutter.

His command was quickly executed, and the schooner's speed was every moment quickening under the additional canvass that had been set—her two enormously-large topsails.

Lightly and swiftly the "Sea Swallow" danced over the sparkling water, and seemed to spurn the waves that buoyed her, as she glided over them now with a speed that seemed to mock the wind.

As the topsails were loosed, a second gun was fired from the cutter, shotted, but the shot passed astern of the schooner, to leeward.

"That fellow had better save his powder, and his credit, if he has any for sailing," said the officer of the schooner, in a lively tone, as he saw the distance between the two vessels was already increased.

On sailed the pirate schooner, and every moment widened the distance between her and the cutter, which still held on in pursuit.

On and on sailed the two vessels for hours, the schooner gaining every hour, till at length the cutter appeared but a speck in the distance, and before the sun had dipped in the blue ocean, was lost to sight.

The schooner held on her course with undiminished speed through the night, till the sun lighted the eastern horizon and ushered in the morn, throwing his fiery spears of light across the vast blue expanse of waters.

After a short run, the "Sea Swallow" was coursing the dark waters of the Mexican Gulf, which she had often scoured under the black flag, and proved a terror to its waters.

After a short cruise here, her course was laid across the Atlantic, and for eight months did the "Sea Swallow" scour its waters, from the Mexican Gulf to the British Channel, along the Spanish and French coasts, under the black flag, which ever waved its gloomy folds aloft.

Her captures were many, and among them several richly-laden Spanish ships, which yielded rich booty to their captor.

Yet never was blood shed unnecessarily, or violence ever offered by any of the crew of the "Sea Swallow" when a prize was captured. Whatever was wanted was taken, and the vessel was then allowed to depart, without further molestation.

It was one fair mild morning, after a three days' run from the English Channel, that a sail was reported from the look-out, two points on the starboard bow, bearing down.

"What do you make her out, Mr. Covell?" asked the captain of the "Sea Swallow" of his officer, who was viewing the approaching sail through a glass.

"A topsail schooner, armed, her decks crowded with men, sir," answered the officer.

"Give me the glass, Mr. Covell," said the captain, quickly.

The glass was handed him, and springing into the main rigging, he levelled it at the stranger.

"He's a saucy-looking chap," said he, after a moment's scrutiny, "and sails under a flag of his own. He carries twelve guns, and a crew of a hundred men, I should guess," said the captain, as he descended from the rigging. "'Two of a trade can never agree,' is the saying."

"Clear away, and get the men ready for action, Mr. Covell. I shall fight that fellow."

The two schooners rapidly neared each other, and

THE APPEAL.

very soon were within gun-shot, when the stranger fired a shot over the bows of the "Sea Swallow," and at the same moment a square of black bunting rose from her deck, and floated at her mast head.

"I guessed aright, Mr. Covell," said the captain, as he beheld the black flag. "Return the compliment, and run up our flag instantly," he said.

The long thirty-two-pounder which the "Sea Swallow carried was got ready, and brought to bear upon the stranger, which had now fallen off, and lay broadside to.

"Give him a shot, any where, and pay off, quickly, Mr. Covell; he must not rake us."

The seaman, who stood ready by the gun with a lighted match, applied it to the powder, at the command of the captain.

The shot took effect in the bulwarks of the stranger, on his starboard bow, throwing the splinters in every direction, and, striking the foremast, knocked a large splinter from it, and went crashing through the larboard bulwarks.

The schooner was instantly brought round, and the two vessels now lay broadside to each other.

"A good shot, two inches more on his bow, would have brought down his foremast," said the captain of the "Sea Swallow."

"Now a broadside, my lads!"

Hardly had the command left his lips, when the vessel shook beneath the shock of the five guns, heavily charged; and simultaneously came the broadside of the stranger, grape-shot and canister, which stretched several of the crew upon the deck; among them was Covell, who was struck by a grape-shot in the forehead, and instantly killed.

After the two broadsides, the two schooners changed their positions, and each, by skilful manœuvring for some time, strove to gain a position to rake the other. But neither could gain the advantage of the other, till, when by a shot from the "Sea Swallow's" long thirty-two, fired by Wing, the foremast of the stranger fell by the board, thus leaving him completely in the power of the other.

A loud cheer rose from the crew of the "Sea Swallow," and broadside after broadside was poured into the other, till the black flag was struck. The "Sea Swallow" was now laid alongside the beaten pirate, which had surrendered, and lay almost a complete wreck upon the water. Nearly half her crew lay dead upon her deck, presenting a horrible and bloody sight.

The captain was the first to board her, followed by Wing, and a score of others.

"Where's the captain of this craft?" asked the captain of the "Sea Swallow" of a seaman, as he gained the deck.

"There he lies," was the answer of the man, pointing to a gigantic corpse upon the deck, but a few paces distant.

"Dead," said the captain, merely bestowing one glance at the corpse.

"Yes, and you lay with him!" were the words of a fierce pirate, who suddenly sprang upon the captain with a raised cutlass, which would have buried itself deep in his brain, but for the timely discharge of a pistol fired by Wing, which laid the pirate a corpse upon the deck.

The captain, not the least unnerved by the sudden attack and imminent danger that had threatened him the instant before, turned calmly round, and saw who had saved him.

He then spoke in a lively tone, "Come, my lads, below! this fellow has gold and silver aboard, and we must have it."

Hardly had the words left his lips, when the cry of "A sail!" was heard from the look-out of his own craft.

"Where away?" he shouted.

"On our lee beam," returned the look-out.

"What do you make her out?" was the inquiry of the captain, in a loud voice.

"A frigate, under full sail. I should judge her to be French," was the answer of the look-out.

The captain sprang into the rigging with a glass, and for a moment scanned the approaching sail. "Yes, she is a French frigate, standing directly for us," he said, as he descended.

"Down into the cabin, some of you, quickly; we must not lose all this treasure! There is undoubtedly treasure there. Down, quickly!"

Half a score of men descended into the cabin of the captured pirate schooner, at the imperative command of the captain, and in a few moments reappeared with three iron chests, which were quickly transferred to the deck of the "Sea Swallow."

There was no time to lose for more treasure; the frigate was within gun-shot, and coming up rapidly. "Fire her!" was the command of the captain, as the three chests were deposited upon the deck of his own vessel.

"If we must lose her treasure, the Frenchman shall not be master of it."

His command was obeyed; the schooner was fired in a dozen places, and the "Sea Swallow" was cleared from her.

As the captain had ordered the other schooner to be fired, he was importuned by the pirates to be taken on board, and not left to be captured by the French.

"Not a mother's son of you. Take to your boats, they will not know your profession," was the answer of the captain.

They were forced to comply with this, the only alternative in their power, and left the burning vessel in the boats, which, luckily for them, were not damaged.

"Tell them any story you like," shouted the captain of the "Sea Swallow," as his vessel put off from the burning wreck.

The French frigate stood on towards the burning vessel, till within hailing distance, when the schooner blew up.

The boats' crews were taken aboard the frigate, which now stood on after the "Sea Swallow," in chase, which proved a fruitless one.

The schooner, but little injured during the engagement with the other pirate, danced as lightly and swiftly over the waves as ever, and every moment left her pursuer farther behind, following on in useless chase.

For a number of days the schooner held on over the ocean, her course laid for the Isle of Pines, the rendezvous of the pirates of the "Sea Swallow."

CHAPTER VI.

THE CAPTAIN'S HISTORY—THE EXPLOSION.

IT was a lovely night as the schooner lay becalmed on the Bahama banks, that the captain sent for Wing to join him in the cabin. The captain had formed a warm attachment for Wing, for the zeal with which he had from the first displayed in his service; but more particularly on account of his life being saved by the young man, whom he had made his first officer after the death of Covell.

As Wing entered the cabin, there was a look of disquietude upon his face, and he cast an apprehensive glance at the captain, who noticed his look of uneasiness, and questioned him respecting it, but received an evasive reply. There was a look of seriousness in the face of the captain not usual in the least to him. He motioned Wing to be seated, and in a tone suited to the serious expression of his face, he spoke—

"Wing, I have called you here to tell you what I never told to mortal ears. What I have to say respects myself. You have several times expressed a desire to know more of my former life; and I promised some time or other to gratify your wishes. I will now briefly relate to you the circumstances which made me what I am. I will pass over the first twenty years of my life, as nothing transpired during that time worthy of note. My parents were wealthy; two sons, an elder brother and myself, were their only children. At twenty years of age I entered the U. S. Navy. I was betrothed to a young and beautiful girl, whom I loved as I believed none could love. I loved the fair girl with the deepest, purest love that ever human heart possessed—idolized her. Her image was ever in my mind—the adored one ever in my thoughts. I was happy in loving such a being, and thrice happy with her love. We were betrothed— the fair girl my affianced bride. Our plighted vows went up to heaven—to the throne of God. I left her with a heart full of sorrow, at the thought of three years' absence; yet there was a bright vision of hallowed love and happiness to come, that cheered me at parting. During that three years' absence, that bright vision was constantly before me. I returned with a heart full of love to throw myself at the feet of the fair being who had inspired me with such love —love that knew no bounds. But, alas! the bright vision that had ever been in my mind—the bright dreams that had ever crowned my hours of sleep, were broken, crushed, vanished for ever. She whom I so madly loved—for whose smile I would have become a slave at her feet, had I been a king—she whom I returned to wed, was in her grave.

"Imagine, if you can—but no, no human heart can imagine the agony, madness, despair, that filled my soul! No human mind could paint the feelings that possessed my soul, when I learned she had died in shame—a victim to the allurements of a villain—a fiend. Oh! did I not swear to Heaven, upon her grave, to have fearful vengeance upon him who had been the destroyer? I did. I kept the oath. That villain was my *brother*. I charged him with the foul, unhallowed crime—no, no, it was no *crime*—deed, He did not deny it. He smiled at my agony; it was the smile of a fiend. He mocked me with his dispassionate words. But his moments were numbered. With a curse, a withering curse upon his soul, I laid that brother a corpse at the feet of his parents and mine. I laughed to see him dead, and only wished that he could again live, that I might again end that life. I stood there his murderer—mine was a crime, his was no crime. It was no crime to destroy both body and soul, one of the fairest creatures that Heaven ever inspired with mortal life—this was no *crime*.

"To rid the world of one who would do this, is a crime that must forfeit life. But had I a thousand lives it would not have deterred me from my oath of vengeance. I sent that brother's guilty soul to be judged at the bar of Almighty God. I was tried for the crime, condemned, and sentenced to death. I escaped from prison, and baffled the strictest search which was made for me. I escaped to sea, and for five years followed it, when the vessel I was in was captured by this one, the "Sea Swallow." Indifferent as to what became of me, reckless of everything, without a tie to bind me to the world, I joined the pirates, and soon became their chief.

"After I had killed my brother, and my thoughts reverted to her who had been his victim, I was seized with a fit of madness; and for two days I was a raving maniac. It is ten years this very night since I committed that deed, and nine times have I been a raving maniac. Every successive year, at the very hour I took that villain's life, has reason fled its throne for the space of one, two, or three hours, or a day. When the hands of the dial of this watch point the hour of twelve, it is ten years since that night, and I shall be for the tenth time a madman. I am confident of it, I know it. As sure as there is a God in Heaven it will be so. It lacks but five short minutes of that hour. Wing, I love you; you saved my life, though I wish you had not, I have a mind to say. Quit this vessel instantly, or in my madness I may do you harm. In these mad fits I have several times attempted the lives of some of my best men. Our best friends in madness appear as greatest foes. Go, quickly, or I cannot answer for what may occur. Take a boat alone, and put off from the schooner till morning; if nothing happens, return. Off!"

The captain seized Wing by the arm, and pushed him toward the cabin-door as he spoke. Wing gazed for a moment into his face, the muscles of which seemed to twitch with convulsive agony. The sweat stood upon his face in beaded drops; a fearful wildness gleamed in his fine dark eyes, and from between his firmly closed lips oozed out white foam. His appearance was terrible.

Wing gazed but a moment at the pirate-chief, then broke from his convulsive grasp upon his arm, and sprang from the cabin and the madman. As he reached the deck, he ordered a boat to be lowered, and, jumping into it quickly, pushed off from the schooner, speaking no word to any on board. He pulled away some distance, and then ceased rowing, and the boat lay motionless upon the calm water. He lay off for nearly an hour, when he resolved to return, and accccordingly put about and pulled towards the schooner.

When within hailing distance, a sudden sound, like a heavy peal of thunder, broke upon the stillness of the night. So sudden, so loud and deafening, was the thunder-like sound, that Wing for a moment was stunned, and rendered almost senseless.

Simultaneously with the report a vivid flash illumined the dark waters for an instant. Then came a fearful crashing sound, like strong timber rent asunder; then sudden, wild, and fearful yells of agony filled the air, startling and terrible. The "Sea Swallow" had blown up!

The air was filled with fragments of the wreck, and human forms were hurled high upward, and fell lifeless into the dark waters.

Wing stood like a statue in the boat; he seemed paralysed at his narrow escape from the sudden and awful doom of the pirate schooner and her crew. His eyes for an instant were turned upward. High above him he beheld a dark object, which seemed directly over him. He heard a rushing sound through the air, as of a falling substance. With an involuntary exclamation of fearful utterance, he dived from the boat far down into the dark water. Hardly had he sank beneath the surface when there was a crash; the boat was crushed to fragments by a heavy timber, the dark body Wing had seen above him, and from which he had barely escaped by diving into the water —a second narrow escape from a terrible death. As he rose to the surface, he could not suppress an involuntary exclamation of joy at his narrow escape from an instantaneous death. At the same instant he felt himself seized by his clothes and drawn under the water for a moment. His first thought was a terrible one—that he was seized by a shark!

But he had become aware in a moment that it was a human being. He strove to free himself from the drowning man, but in vain; his grasp was like iron in its hold. He sought for his dagger, which he always carried about him, and which he found in a moment, and with it he cut one of the hands that had seized him from the wrist, and with a sudden plunge he freed himself from the death grasp of the drowning man, who sank to rise no more. Wing now struck out for some spar or piece of wreck whereby to sustain himself, and soon succeeded in getting upon a large portion of the blown-up schooner, where he remained till morning.

The sun rose red in the east, and threw his beams of golden hue over the blue water, now slightly rippled by a gentle breeze which had sprung up as the day broke upon the broad blue ocean. Wing gazed around him o'er the sunlit water, in hope that a sail might gladden his anxious sight; but he could discover none. Nought met his eye but the fragments of the schooner, that strewed the sea around him—all that remained of the once beautiful "Sea Swallow." And he alone, of all her crew, that had escaped her terrible fate, stood there near the scene of her destruction, upon a fragment of the deck of the schooner.

Wing had kept the hand he had cut from the wrist of the drowning man, and at the first light of morn he discovered, by a ring upon one of the fingers, that it was the hand of Harding. He cut the ring, which was set with a magnificent diamond, from the stiffened and tightly-closed finger, and then tossed the bloody hand from him.

"Poor Ned! he's gone!" he murmured, in a tone of pity, at the thoughts of his friend's fate. He remained for some time buried in deep and heaving thought. At length a sudden, bitter imprecation burst from his lips.

"Curses on my fortune! Thus it is ever with me; always foiled in my designs. Had it not been for this affair, the "Sea Swallow," ere to-morrow night, would have been mine. Would to God I had struck this steel to his heart last night! I should have been chief of the pirates now—should have saved the schooner from destruction, and led the free life of the rover. But she is gone! the beautiful craft, with all her treasure, which now lies beneath me, buried for ever!"

Wing, as he stood upon the rocking fragment, seemed almost overpowered by the feelings of deep and bitter disappointment that filled his breast, and he uttered curse upon curse.

He had conceived a plan for murdering the captain, taking the schooner, and proclaiming himself captain of her. He had, by bribing and liberal promises to them, gained nearly half the crew to his purpose, and the next night was to be the time of execution of their plan; but the destruction of the schooner frustrated his design. He stood crushed to the soul with the disappointment, and he gave vent to his feelings in bitter and malignant oaths.

Hour after hour passed on, and he watched anxiously for the appearance of a sail. His situation was anything but an agreeable one; exposed to the burning rays of the sun, the fierce heat of which almost overpowered him, as he stood without the least shelter from the intense heat.

In the flashing water he could see, playing around the piece of wreck he stood upon, a number of sharks—those terrible monsters of the deep. He could see their flashing sides as they darted around him, sometimes half out of the water, greedy for a victim upon which to feast their voracious appetites.

A terrible feast these monsters had had the night before, of human beings! Wing imagined what a horrible death would be his if he were to throw himself into the water; and he could not but feel grateful at his escape from their ravenous jaws.

The hours passed on, and no sail hove in sight to gladden his anxious eye. Night came, shrouding the ocean with its mantle of darkness, and not a speck was visible to the eye.

It was a long, long night to Wing; he wished it day, and yet he dreaded the fierce heat that day would bring. Morn at length broke, and the fierce red sun rose from out the blue sea, and the rippling waves flashed brightly in the fiery light.

Higher and higher rose the sun, and fiercer grew his burning rays. Wing writhed in agony beneath the merciless heat of the fiery orb. He gazed around upon the flashing ocean, but nothing like a sail was visible to his eye. The day passed, and another night came.

Slowly the long hours of the night passed to him. He could not sleep; he dared not risk to close his eyes upon the frail fragment that bore him, for fear of the terrible monsters around him. Slowly indeed passed the tedious hours of that night, till the morn again broke.

That day passed, and Wing, groaning under the broiling heat of the sun, suffered dreadful agony till night again closed around him, without a sail appearing in sight. The minutes seemed hours to him throughout that long night, in his agony and despair. But day once more broke, and the red light of the sun gleamed over the blue ocean, which seemed to welcome the fiery mantle. It was the fourth morn since the destruction of the schooner, and Wing was almost overcome by the horrible situation he was in.

The hours passed till noon, and the fierce rays of the sun shed down upon him seemed more intense than ever, and caused him more excruciating pain. To add to this burning torture, hunger was gnawing him, increasing his agony most terribly, and his intense thirst rendered him almost a madman. He gazed around over the blazing ocean in agony of despair; but no sail met his longing gaze. His face was stamped with the wild despair that filled his soul at his horrible situation. A dreadful fate stared him in the face—a lingering death by starvation threatened inevitably to be his, far more terrible than the death he had escaped by the blowing up of the schooner.

From hunger and thirst he suffered the greatest agony. He bathed his parched lips as he knelt with the salt water, and swallowed the warm salt liquid down his burning throat; but this increased his thirst tenfold; yet he drank it, for it moistened his parched mouth and throat.

He gazed into the lurid water, and beheld a score of sharks darting around him; and he seemed to deliberate upon throwing himself among them and ending his horrible suffering; but a sense of the dreadful death deterred him. Yet, on the other hand, a far more dreadful, more lingering death awaited him by starvation. He groaned aloud in agony at the torture he suffered, and there was a wild and fearful expression upon his haggard face that was truly terrible.

The sun poured down his fierce heat-piercing rays upon him, and he became almost a raving madman under the excruciating torture. Dreadful indeed were his sufferings from hunger and thirst, and the burning heat of the sun—indescribable. Nature could not much longer sustain herself under such torture.

That day passed, and another night. Though during the night he was relieved of one torture, the broiling heat of the sun, yet he suffered from the dreadful gnawings of hunger and burning thirst, which seemed consuming him inwardly. He would have given worlds for the hand which he had cut from the drowning man, and which he had cast away, to have it now, that he might gnaw the flesh from the bones and somewhat appease his raving hunger; and for one draught of water he would have bartered away his soul.

The fifth morn at length broke, and the red sun again rose from out the blue ocean up into the clear blue heavens, with not a cloud to obscure the fiery brilliancy of the burning orb of day. A strong wind now swept the ocean, and the ruffled waves danced and flashed in the red light of the sun like waves of fire.

Wing hailed the light of day, yet he fearfully dreaded its heat. He gazed with straining eyes around and around the horizon's circle for the appearance of a sail; but he was doomed to disappointment. With an oath of wild despair he clutched his dagger, and raised it above his breast for a blow. For an instant he hesitated, and his arm fell powerless to his side. The love of life deterred him from striking the blow; he yet had hopes of being saved. He took in his hand some water to wet his parched lips, when a sudden thought seemed to strike him. He stripped his left arm bare, and with his dagger he made a deep incision, to which he applied his parching lips and drank his hot red blood till he sickened of the taste.

The time passed on till the sun betokened the hour of noon; the burning heat, shed relentlessly upon, had nearly overcome Wing, who lay in his agony upon the fragment of the wreck, wishing for death to end his sufferings.

His eyes, which from the first light of day had scanned the ocean, were of a sudden directed in a quarter where in the azure distance of the horizon appeared a white speck, like a white cloud on the ocean's verge. His eyes were fixed intently upon the distant speck, which every moment grew larger and larger to the gaze. He knew it was a sail; and his spirits, which had well nigh fled, now seemed revived within him at the joyful hopes of deliverance.

Larger and larger appeared the sail every moment to his eye, and his gaze grew more and more intent. His eyes seemed starting from their sockets in their intense and fixed gaze. He made out the distant but approaching sail to be a ship, standing directly for him.

His face expressed a wild and frantic joy as he gazed at the approaching sail. He felt not the burning heat of the noon-day sun; he felt no hunger, no thirst, so absorbed was his soul by the prospect of deliverance from his horrible situation.

The ship bore up till within two miles, when her course was changed, and it was evident to Wing she would sail directly by him. Horror and despair seized his soul as he observed this, and a piercing, agonizing cry burst from his lips. With the strength that this despair imparted to him he rose to his feet, and tearing from his neck the black kerchief he wore, waved it in the wind for a number of minutes, when his signal was discovered on board the ship, which tacked and bore up for him. The despair of Wing now gave way to frantic joy, and overpowered by his feelings he sank down and lay lifeless upon the fragment that for five days had borne him upon the water.

CHAPTER V.

THE OUTCAST.

WE will now change the scene to the mansion of Mr. Wing, at a period three years after the events related in the foregoing chapter.

It was evening. Mr. Wing sat in his splendidly furnished parlor, and near him, upon a sofa, sat a female whose age might have been two and twenty years. Her face, though pale, and somewhat shrunken from a former roundness, plainly showed that beauty, —matchless beauty, once was hers. Deep melancholy rested upon her pale face, and told that some deep seated grief which preyed within had robbed her, in a great degree, of the beauty she once possessed. Beside her upon the sofa, asleep, with his head in her lap, was a fair-haired, handsome boy, of some three or four summers, and whose features very much resembled those of the female, who affectionately caressed the young child as he slept, and tears fell from her eyes as she gazed fondly upon the sleeping boy.

A tear unbidden moistened the eye of Mr. Wing, as he gazed at the sorrowing mother and her beautiful child. He had evidently been conversing respecting his long absent son, for he now spoke.

"No, Eliza, I would not care ever to see his face again, were it not for your sake, and the sake of your sleeping innocent. Where he is, whether dead or alive, Heaven only knows! Deeply as you feel the sorrow which weighs so heavily upon your heart, I feel it as keenly as yourself, as deeply! But hark! I hear heavy footsteps upon the stairway; we have a visitor unannounced!"

As he spoke, the door opened, and Willard Wing stood before them, who, as his eye fell upon the sofa, seemed struck with utter amazement. He stood like one confounded, as his gaze was riveted upon her. Like a statue he stood, as immoveable!

An instant, and a wild scream burst from the lips of the young female, as she sprang towards him and clasped her arms about his neck, imprinting upon his face a torrent of kisses in her wild joy, and exclaimed in a voice of heartfelt joy—

"Oh, Willard, Willard, is this indeed you? Do I again behold you? clasp you in these arms? Oh, Heaven, I am indeed once more happy."

Her head fell upon his neck, and she wept for very joy.

A frown blacker than midnight shadowed the brow of Wing, as he stood with his neck encircled by the arms of the weeping woman.

His eye shot forth a fierce, angry gleam; and his face expressed the deepest rage and mortification.

He forced her clasped hands apart, and pushed her from him, and exclaimed in a tone of brutal feeling, "What means this? Who are you, woman?"

She knelt at his feet, clasped one of his hands within hers, and fixed her full, dark eye, suffused with tears, upon him.

"Oh, Willard, Willard, do not talk thus," she exclaimed, in a heart-breaking tone of anguish. "You know me. Oh, say you know your once loved Eliza— her you once loved, who so fondly loved you, who loves you now, and ever shall. Oh, do not look so cruelly upon me—do not, or my heart will break. For God's sake, Willard, look more kindly on me—look at me as you once looked, with love beaming in your eyes. Look upon that sleeping, innocent boy, your son! Oh, will you not love him, the beautiful boy. I will awaken him, that his eyes for the first time may behold his father. Oh, you will love him, Willard, your darling boy!"

She awoke the rosy-cheeked, handsome child, who, as he awoke, fixed his full, beautiful blue eye, radiant with happiness, upon her, and with a merry laugh, threw his arms about his mother's neck, and kissed her. She clasped him to her bosom, and imprinted upon his fine brow sweet kisses, and her eye told how deep was that mother's love for her lovely child.

"Come Willard, you shall see your father. There he is—run to him, kiss him, child."

The fond mother motioned him to Wing, and the child ran toward him, stretching up his little hands, exclaiming in a musical voice, "Papa, papa, I kiss you?" and the little fellow, with his pretty mouth ready to bestow the kiss, strove to pull himself up to his father's face.

The mother had hoped to reach the heart of Wing through her lovely child, but she was bitterly disappointed. He bestowed an angry scowl upon the child, and said in a harsh and cruel tone.

"Away, brat, go to your mother, if she is your mother." The little fellow turned from him, while his full blue eyes filled with tears, and ran to his mother, who caught him up in her arms, while from her eyes also fell scalding tears. "Papa scold me; papa wont let me kiss," uttered the little fellow, with a sob as if his heart would break.

The mother said not a word, but wept with her lovely boy.

"The furies seize her!" muttered Wing, to himself, grinding his teeth with rage, as he gazed at the sorrowing mother, who had now seated herself with her sobbing child clasped to her breast.

"What means this? can you inform me, sir?" was the inquiry of Wing, turning to his father, to whom he had not spoken till now.

His father looked sternly upon him for several moments, and then in a sterner tone said—

"Young man, this subterfuge is vain. Think not to deceive me by your pretended ignorance of this young woman. I know all. I have learned all concerning you during the year and a half you were absent from here, as I thought at college. I have learned of the short stay you made there, and of your conduct while there. I know of your expulsion from the University, three months after you entered there, and of the dissolute life you afterwards led in Boston, till you were forced to relinquish your sinful pleasures by my refusal to send you the wherewithal to gratify them. I know the story of this sorrowing young woman; of the foul, base wrong you have done her. Oh, God! that a son of mine should be a wretch so guilty."

The father uttered this in a voice choked with grief and hot tears of sorrow fell from his eyes. He grew calmer in a moment, when he again spoke.

"For her sake, my son, I forgive you all this, on condition you make her the only reparation in your power for the base wrong you have done her. Wed her this very night, and I forgive you, as she does. Otherwise you go from this house a beggar, with a father's curse upon your head. Do you consent? Let me have your answer."

The son, who had regarded him while he spoke with mingled looks of anger and chagrin, now spoke in a tone of affected carelessness—

"Why, then, sir, if you know all, there is no use of further concealment. But as to wedding her, why, I have already done that; she is my wife, sir."

"Would you seek to deceive me further?" said the father, sternly. "It was a mock marriage, young man, a false marriage! and I know of the base associate of yours who conspired with you to deceive this young woman, and who performed the marriage rites—profaned those sacred rites. You cannot deny it—you dare not."

"I do not care to deny it, sir, since you know it," said the son, in a reckless tone. "But wed her again, I will not, sir," he again said, in a determined tone, while his eye flashed defiance at his father.

"Then you are no longer a son of mine. I renounce you to the world, as one of the basest villains it contains. But no! you shall wed her this very hour."

The father spoke this in a stern, determined manner, and as he spoke advanced toward his son, and whispered in his ear. The son started back, fixed his dark eyes upon his father with astonishment. His heaving chest told that the whispered words had touched a chord of sensitive feeling within.

"Wed her, or this shall be known," said the father sternly, in an under tone.

"I will, if you swear to keep the secret, sir," said the son, after a moment's hesitation.

"I will not expose you, my word for it," said Mr. Wing; and as he spoke he rang for an attendant. His summons was soon obeyed, and a neatly clad young man made his appearance, to whom Mr. Wing whispered a few words, and the young man departed. Half an hour afterwards a clergyman was announced, and ushered into the parlor; and in a few moments Willard Wing and Eliza Moulton were united in marriage.

As soon as he had performed the ceremony, the clergyman departed, and a moment after, without uttering a word, young Wing also left the room.

During the interval between the departure of the servant and the arrival of the clergyman, Mr. Wing had been remonstrating with his son against the dissolute life he had lived, and strenuously urged him to abandon it, and reform his ways. He told him of the certain ruin and ignominy that would sooner or later inevitably overtake him if he persisted in his abandoned way of living. He pictured to him the unbounded happiness that he might enjoy in the society of his beautiful boy, and the lovely woman before him, when wedded to her.

But his remonstrances, and the vivid picture of happiness, which he drew with intensity of feeling, produced no effect upon his son, callous to every sense of propriety, and Mr. Wing gave up the task in despair.

Three months from that wedding night, the wife of young Wing was a corpse. The cruel neglect of her husband, who took not the slightest notice of her or her beautiful child, preyed upon her mind, and her constitution, already impaired by grief, that ravisher of health, rapidly gave way under the continued sorrow, and she died, breathing a prayer for him who had been the destroyer of her happiness, and the cause of her premature death.

Her death, instead of inflicting any sorrow upon Wing, rather rejoiced him; he seemed relieved of a burden to his existence.

Mr. Wing, incensed beyond all bearing at the unnatural and cruel conduct of his son, turned him out of his house, with an injunction never to enter it again unless as a better man.

The young man heard his father in sullen silence, and departed from the house without any manifestations whatever of regret at leaving.

Thus young Wing left his father's house, an outcast; left a home where he might have lived as happy a life as ever fell to the lot of mortal.

But perhaps the reader would like to know what happened to young Wing after being rescued from the situation we left him in at the close of the last chapter, until he made his appearance at his father's house. We will in few words relate what befel him.

Taken from the piece of wreck insensible, it was some time before he recovered from the almost fatal effects of the exposure and suffering he had endured. The ship which had reached him was a West Indiaman, bound to Liverpool. At that port, having perfectly recovered, Wing left the ship, and but a few nights after was taken by a press-gang, and conveyed aboard of an English man-of-war, then lying in port. He was two years and a half in this man-of-war, when he and a number of others were transferred to the British frigate "Guerriere," which was shortly afterwards captured by the U. S. frigate "Constitution." Shortly after the capture he returned home.

At a late hour one night, three weeks after his banishment from home, Wing stood at a billiard table engaged in play with a young man. Wing excelled at billiards; he loved the game. He had that evening been the victor of nine successive games with the young man with whom he was now playing the tenth.

A group around the table watched the players with interest, as each tried their utmost to gain the advantage. After some time, Wing proved himself victor again. The tenth game was his. Dashing his cue with an oath violently upon the table, his opponent exclaimed, with petulance, that he had played unfair.

"You are a liar!" exclaimed Wing, fiercely. "You have lost, and now would reproach me with playing unfair. You are a liar, and you know it. There is your money back, if you think I played unfair, baby!"

Wing uttered this in a contemptuous, sneering tone, as he threw down upon the table five hundred dollars he had won.

Quicker than thought his antagonist sprang across the table, and struck him a blow in the forehead that felled him to the floor, where for a moment he lay senseless. It was but a moment ere he recovered and sprang to his feet.

"By Jove!" he exclaimed, fiercely, "I'll have your heart's blood for that!"

With a fearful expression of murderous meaning upon his face, he sprang toward the young man, and seizing him by the throat with an iron-like gripe, drew from beneath his vest a small dirk, and ere any could stay his hand, he plunged the weapon to its hilt into the breast of the young man, who uttered a groan and fell to the floor.

Ere any one could detain him, Wing fled from the room and gained the street. He crossed to the opposite side of the street, which lay in shadows as the moon was setting, and away along the darkened side he ran with the greatest rapidity.

Once only he looked around as he was about to

THE MURDER OF THE OLD CLOTHES-SALESMAN.

turn down a narrow and obscure street; he saw no one in pursuit as he turned into it, and he proceeded yet as rapidly as before. This street led to the water, and was lined on either side by poor, miserable, crazy-looking buildings.

Along this street on the darkened side Wing flew like the wind, till he nearly reached the end, when he stopped before one of the craziest of the crazy-looking buildings, and knocked sharply at the door.

"Who's there?" squeaked a voice within, after Wing had knocked three several times.

"It's me, Jones. Let me in quickly."

"Don't know you; sha'n't let you in," answered the voice within.

"If you don't, I'll stave your crazy door down," said Wing fiercely, in reply.

"Stave away, and I'll stave your brains out," said the voice, in return.

"Here goes then! I'll risk my brains," said Wing, as he stepped a little back, as if to throw himself against the door. Just then, he observed, on the opposite side of the way, a little distance off, a seaman in company with a female who had just accosted him. The seaman had stopped, and for a moment was in conversation with the female, when he suddenly left her, and strode with a rapid pace away.

But he was followed by the female, who caught hold of him and stopped him.

In an instant he broke from her, but was again seized by the female.

"That's Marshall! I wonder what she is hanging round him for?" said Wing, to himself.

"Ha! He stabs her. She falls!"

As he spoke, the female fell to the pavement, uttering a groan, and the seaman fled rapidly away.

Wing started as if to go towards the fallen woman, but immediately stopped.

"No, I'll not trouble her," he said. "If I should happen to be caught with her, I should have to father that murder also. One is enough for to-night. But old Jones must let me in. I must get a seaman's dress, and be off before sunrise."

As he spoke, he again knocked at the door of the old clothes-vendor's shop.

"Let me in, Jones, I want to buy of you."

The door was opened as he spoke this, and he entered the place. It was a small shop, thickly lined on either side with old clothes and new, of all shapes and sizes.

The proprietor of this extensive establishment was a short, thin-looking specimen of humanity, with a wrinkled and ill-looking visage, which was rendered still more forbidding by a frightful scar that ran from one eye down to the chin.

He slept in the shop upon an old chest, and was roused from his sleep by the knocking of Wing.

"Sorry to wake you, Jones. But come, find me a Jack's dress; I'm off in the morning."

"Show me the color first," said the old clothes-dealer, looking hard at him.

"You old skinflint! I've got money enough to pay for them," said Wing, sharply. "Find the clothes that will fit me, and you have the money. Come, Jerry, be spry."

"What, do you want a whole rig-out?" asked Jerry.

"Yes."

"Roundabout, trousers, blue shirt, handkerchief, slippers, tarpaulin—"

"Yes, all these, and an old wig, if you've got one."

"Why, what the devil are you up to, Wing," asked the clothes dealer. "A wig! What do you want of a wig?—ha—ha!—I've got a red wig here. You shall have it; it'll look so becoming. You with a red wig on?—ha—ha—ha! What a figure-head."

"Jerry, you are inclined to be merry; but hang the wig, get me the clothes, and then I'll look at the red-top."

In a few moments Wing was dressed in a neat and well-fitting seaman's attire.

"Now for the wig, Jerry," said he, laughing.

From the bottom of an old box the clothes-dealer hauled out the red wig, and fiery red it was.

Wing took it and fixed it on his head, and upon it he placed the tarpaulin.

The disguise was most complete. The little old clothes-dealer laughed quite heartily.

None of his most intimate friends would have recognized Wing, so altered in appearance by the red, shaggy-looking wig.

"Should you know me, Jerry?"

"Not I, nor the devil, your best friend," answered the clothes-dealer, laughing. "But, Wing, what is this all about? Got into a row, and goin' to run, 'spose?"

"Oh, I gave a fellow six inches of cold steel, that's all," said Wing, carelessly, in reply.

"Let daylight into him, eh! Did you kill him?"

"Made a hole in him."

"What are you goin' to do?"

"Ship to-morrow morning in the Chesapeake. But come, see how much I owe you?"

Jerry, with a huge piece of chalk, now began to reckon up the amount upon the blackened counter.

"Seventy dollars for the whole," he said, in a moment. "It's cheap."

"Seventy dollars, you infernal Jew! Do you suppose I shall give you that for these clothes?"

"Or leave 'em," said the clothes-dealer, indifferently.

He meant to take good advantage of the situation of Wing, who he knew must have the clothes.

"You ought to have been born a Jew, Jerry. You think to take advantage of me, but you don't, my old one. Here's thirty dollars for the clothes; they never cost you twenty."

"Give me my price, or you can't have the clothes."

"I've got them on; I should like to see you take them off, Jerry! Good bye, I'm off!"

"Give me the seventy dollars, Wing, or I'll blow," said Jerry, as Wing stood with his hand upon the latch of the door.

"You will, will you? you miserable earth-worm! You'll blow about my shipping, will you?"

"Yes, I will, d—n you!" squeaked out Jerry.

"Do you mean that, Jerry?" asked Wing, advancing toward him with a menacing look.

"I do, if you don't pay me the seventy dollars. I'll do it, if I have breath."

"Then I'll stop your breath now, you shadow of nothing!" said Wing, fiercely, as he glanced contemptuously upon the puny form of the man before him. He seized him by the throat and fairly lifted him from his feet, and held him till his face grew livid and his eyes protruded frightfully; and then, with a violent wrench of the hand that grasped the throat of the man, he flung him to the floor. "You would have blown, would you? I doubt whether you will now. It strikes me your windpipe is a trifle damaged—ha, ha!"

There was no remorse betrayed by Wing as he spoke these words. He laughed with satisfaction. Lifting the form of the man he had choked to death, he threw it behind the counter, and extinguishing the candle, left the shop, taking with him the clothes he had worn on first going in, now tied up in a handkerchief.

He walked rapidly down to the dock and tossed the clothes into the water, and then turned his steps back and went rapidly up the street. Turning into Broadway, he bent his steps toward the saloon, from which he had lately fled.

Before the door of the saloon he beheld a carriage drawn up, and as he approached a number of persons emerged from the saloon bearing the body of a man, which they placed in the carriage.

"Halloa, shipmate! what's the matter with that fellow? Too much grog aboard?" asked Wing of a man, whom he approached with a rolling, half-drunken gait.

"No, Jack," answered the man. "He had better have grog aboard of him than what he has. He was dirked up stairs in the billiard-room."

"Who dirked him?"

"A young fellow by the name of Wing. He'll swing if the chap dies."

"If they catch him," said Wing to himself. "He aint a dead man, then?"

"No, he may live, though the chance is a hard one," was the answer, and Wing walked with a rolling gait away.

"I must leave these quarters, for a dead certainty," said he to himself. "The 'Chesapeake' sails to-morrow; she wants seamen. I don't like it; but it's Hobson's choice, and I must take it."

The next morning witnessed the departure of the U. S. frigate "Chesapeake" for New York bay.

Among the seamen in the forecastle were two who stood aloof from the rest in conversation.

"How odd that you and I should be shipmates again!" said one of them to the other.

"But how came you to ship, Wing?"

"Hush, Marshall! my name is Williams here," said the other. "Had a blow up with the old man, my father; spent too much of his money; kicked me out of doors, and so I shipped; but remember my name is Williams."

An order from the officer of the deck at that moment stopped the conversation between Wing and Marshall.

Wing was but one week on board the frigate; and what happened to him has already been related to the reader in his own words, in the second chapter, in his conversation with Mardon, on board the privateer "White Cloud."

CHAPTER VIII.

THE PRIVATEER.

IT was a beautiful morn in October, the air was cool and bracing, the heavens blue and cloudless. The sun was climbing the cloudless heavens, and shedding on earth and ocean its golden light. Over all was the golden mantle spread; on the mansion of the rich man, on the cottage of the poor man. The high mountain, the broad plain, the dark forests, the winding rivers, all looked bright and beautiful in the aureal light of the morning sun. The white crests of the blue heaving waves of the ocean flashed and sparkled in its glowing rays; and the calm inland waters lay like flashing mirrors, reflecting the dazzling radiance of the orb of day.

On this beautiful morn, down the lovely bay of Boston, was gliding one of the most splendid craft that had ever graced the waters of the bay. She was a brigantine under full sail; of a most charming model and beautiful appearance. Her snow-white canvass, piled like a pyramid against her foremast, seemed towering to the heavens. Ten brass guns upon her deck flashed back the dazzling rays of the morning sun, and the highly-polished metal seemed to shoot forth living fire.

At the main peak of the brigantine fluttered the stars and stripes. Proudly waved that flag; proudly, as if conscious and vain of waving from the peak of a craft so beautiful, whose appearance elicited warm praise from the lips of many a rough sailor as she passed swiftly the numerous craft that studded the blue waters of the bay. On she sped till she pressed the bosom of the broad Atlantic, and danced lightly and swiftly over the foam-crested waves of the ocean.

It was a beautiful sight! that gallant craft speeding on, her canvass towering to the skies, and flashing with brilliancy in the red light of the sun! It was a sight to warm the blood, and kindle the eye with admiration! There was a goodly crew upon the deck of the brigantine, as to looks and numbers. Young, brave, and fearless-looking; gallant men they were.

There was one upon her quarter-deck whose eye, as he glanced aloft, bespoke the pride that filled his heart; proud he was of the gallant and beautiful vessel that bore him as its master.

"What think you of our craft, Mr. Wing?" he asked, in a warm tone, as he glanced aloft and alow, with the deepest admiration expressed in his bold and handsome face.

"Well, Captain Seawood, I think she is second to none; equal to any that floats the waves," answered Wing, in a warm, animated tone.

"So do I. She is a beauty! she is a witch! Mr. Wing," said the Captain, in a voice of animation, while his eyes sparkled with pride as he glanced around the deck, and up aloft. "By Heavens! I am as deeply in love with the brigantine, as was ever an enraptured swain with a lovely damsel."

"She is a lovely craft, the White Cloud, Captain," said Wing, as he glanced around. "It is lucky for you and I, Captain, that she is not a woman, for I am as deeply in love with the brigantine as yourself."

"How she sails; how she flies before this catspaw of a breeze! If a spanking wind increase her speed in proportion, there is not a craft that floats that could keep in her wake; nor Lucifer himself rig a craft that could overhaul her."

"I envy you, Captain Seawood, the command of such a craft—on my soul, I do."

"But you have the second, Mr. Wing," said the Captain, smiling.

"Ay, and I am proud of that; but yet I envy you the first. You are a lucky man, Captain Seawood, and yet I do not know that I should grumble, being second in command of such a craft."

"No; but let us below, Wing. But what is that fellow a-head? Get a glass, Wing."

The Captain as he spoke, bent his eyes upon a large vessel that loomed up at some distance right ahead, standing across the bows of the brigantine.

It will be well, perhaps, to inform the reader how Wing came to be on board the "White Cloud," and the second in command.

The berth had been obtained for him by his father, who was a highly esteemed friend of the owners of the brigantine. They had made known to Mr. Wing their enterprise in fitting out the brigantine as a privateer, and he obtained for his son the second command of her. Mr. Wing, in watching over his son during the strange illness that had seized him on board the frigate "Chesapeake," which the reader will recollect was related by Wing in a preceding chapter, had forgotten and forgiven the past conduct of his son, and earnestly besought and prayed him to amend his ways, as he had often prayed in vain before.

The young man whom his son had stabbed, and so nearly robbed of life, in the billiard-room, had recovered, and in consideration of a large amount of money paid him by Mr. Wing, had instituted no proceedings against his son. This was settled to the no small joy of Mr. Wing, who yet had hopes of saving his son from the ignominy and ruin that threatened him inevitably, if he still pursued the career to which he had hitherto abandoned himself. With these hopes in his heart, he had satisfied the young man who had so severely suffered by his son, and he obtained for the latter the situation we have already seen him occupying. But now to the deck of the privateer.

Captain Seawood stood in the fore-rigging, with a glass levelled at the sail a-head.

"By ——! as I hope to live, that fellow is an English sloop-of-war!" exclaimed he, after a few moment's scrutiny. "An English sloop-of-war cruising off Boston! Confound his impudence!" he said, as he jumped to the deck. "Wonder if he will let the 'White Cloud' blow past him?"

"I rather think it will pass two miles astern," said Wing.

"If we both keep our course; but see! the corvette is falling off! She has the wind now on her starboard quarter, as we have, and is three points on our larboard bow, laying her course exactly with ours. That is very odd! A privateer chasing a sloop-of-war—ha, ha! That is rich. But I see—she knows what we are, but thinks we don't know her. I never was so mistaken before, if I don't. She wants us to be neighbourly, come up within gunshot, and then—why, then blow us to the devil. Ha, ha! I think it is very likely she will—not. She is trying to play the Yankee merchantman, Wing; see the stars and stripes going aloft. It won't do, Johnny, the horns will stick out. I'll open a conversation with him through our friend, long Tom. Get it ready for speaking, Wing.'

As the Captain spoke, he again ascended the rigging with his glass, where he stood for some moments. The brigantine was walking rapidly up with the corvette, at a rate that would soon bring the two within gun-shot.

"We can hit now, Captain Seawood," said Wing, addressing his superior.

"We can, but we can go nearer, and still be out of the reach of their guns, and our shot be the more sure," said the Captain, descending to the deck.

A few moments more, and the brigantine was still nearing the sloop-of-war, which was now wearing to windward.

'Now's the time, Wing. I want to see your skill at playing ball. How is the piece?"

Wing glanced his eye along the ponderous gun for a moment, and then said—

"It is too high; the shot will go over her hull. Depress the piece a little, men. There, that will do.

"Put that ball through her bulwarks, just aft the main-mast, if you can, Wing. At all events, put it into the hull somewhere—don't miss. Fire!"

As the Captain gave the word, Wing applied the lighted match. The gun vomited forth the red flame, and its iron messenger flew like lightning across the intervening space of water that separated the brigantine and corvette.

"By—! as I hope to live, you have hit her, Wing, in the very spot I named," said the Captain, who stood in the rigging with his glass. "You have made a pretty hole in her bulwarks; and I am mistaken if you have not scraped her main-mast. You deserve a cheer for that, Wing. A cheer for our gunner, my men, now."

As the Captain spoke, a wild, simultaneous huzza burst from the brigantine's crew, and the shout rang upon the air and was wafted away to the corvette's crew.

"I would like to hear the Englishmen swear," said the Captain, laughing heartily, as the cheer of his crew died away. "Ha—ha—" he laughed, "their curses would sink the brigantine. Ha, there goes her colors, and now she shows her teeth. Now she spits her venom out."

As he spoke, a jet of red flame burst from the bows of the corvette, which had wore round, and was now standing for the brigantine. Her shot fell far short of the intended mark, and sank into the blue water.

"Starboard the helm!" shouted Captain Seawood.

"Starboard it is," answered the helmsman.

"Now fire again, Johnny, do!" said the Captain.

Hardly had the words left his lips, when the red flash again burst from the corvette, and the report of the gun came booming over the water. Again the shot fell far short of the brigantine, which seemed to fly like a bird over the flashing waters.

"They will waste no more powder till they get nearer; and if they wait till then, the probability is, they will keep all they have," said the Captain of the brigantine, while a smile wreathed his lips, and his eye lighted with pride at the consciousness of the superior sailing qualities of his vessel.

On ploughed the stately and gallant brigantine, through the white foam-crested waves, while standing down upon her on her starboard bow was the English corvette, her bows wreathed to the head in the snowy foam.

"We shall have the Englishman on our starboard quarter before he can get within gun-shot," said the Captain of the brigantine to Wing, as his gaze was fixed on the corvette.

"I believe the brigantine would sail round that fellow, let him do his utmost at sailing," said Wing, in a moment after.

Half an hour, and the corvette, as Captain Seawood had said, was on the starboard quarter of the brigantine, standing on; the brigantine running away from her every moment.

Three hours, and the corvette was hull down in the distance, and the pile of snowy canvass looked like a floating cloudlet on the blue verge of the horizon.

CHAPTER IX.

THE PLOT DEFEATED.

WE will not follow the privateer, "White "Cloud," on her first cruise. A year after she sailed she returned to Boston, her cruise having been a very successful one. An hour after she came to anchor at evening, Wing left her for a stroll on shore.

As he was strolling along through a street that intersected the pier where he had landed, and lined on either side by miserable buildings or rather hovels, he suddenly stopped in his walk, and exclaimed, as he gazed at a man who stood in the doorway of the tap-room.

"That is Marshall, sure as death!" and as he spoke he made towards the individual. "Marshall!" he said, in a voice of some surprise.

"Wing!" said the other, with still more surprise, as the two shook each other heartily by the hand.

"Aye, both of us, I guess," said Wing; "but how is it you are here, Marshall?"

"Why, the 'Chesapeake' made a short cruise of

it. She was captured by the 'Shannon' about four months ago. An exchange of prisoners being made, our crew returned to New York, and I started for Boston, sick of a sailor's life in the navy."

"And took up with a business more profitable," said Wing, "but where is that midshipman, Burton?"

"I don't know," answered Marshall; "but come in, and take a drop."

"It will be well for him if I and him never meet," said Wing, as the two entered the tap-room. "And you will be lucky if you get off unscathed, Mike Marshall," muttered he to himself, in a revengeful tone; "to you I owe that whipping I received. But I'll cancel it. But Marshall," he said, again addressing him, "how came you to get hold of this place?"

"My old dad kept it for years; but the old fellow died just after I got home, so I took the business; and, as you say, it is more profitable than to follow the sea. But now about you, let us know?"

Wing now related his adventures to Marshall, briefly.

"And so you are second in command of a privateer?" said Marshall, as Wing concluded.

"Aye, and hope to be first some day," said the latter, in a meaning tone.

"Hope you will be. But what will you drink?"

"Brandy."

"Nance! Nance!" called out Marshall, as he directed his eyes to a door that led into a room at one end of the bar, and which stood open.

Quickly, in obedience to his call, a young girl came from the back room to the bar. The girl was young and handsome, and neatly attired. Wing started, and uttered an involuntary exclamation, as if at beholding one so young and handsome an inmate of a place so vile.

The tap-room of the Best Bower has already been described, as the reader will recollect. The young girl placed two tumblers upon the bar, and asked what they would drink.

"I'll have brandy, my pretty maid," said Wing, as he gazed at her steadily, till her face flushed to a crimson hue. "That brandy tastes the better for your mixing, my little beauty," said he, as he swallowed the liquor.

Placing the tumbler upon the bar, he bent over and bestowed a kiss upon the fair face of the young girl, who reddened to the brow at the unexpected salute. But quicker than thought she struck him a smart blow in the face with the back of her hand, and then disappeared into the back room.

"She has got spirit," said he, laughing at the rebuff he had received from the young girl. "Who is that young girl, Mike?" he asked of Marshall, who stood laughing quite heartily at the reception Wing had received in return for his kiss.

"That is my sister, and you see you must not be too familiar on a short acquaintance."

"I am sensible of that, quite," said Wing, whose face yet tingled from the smart blow he had received. "A sister of yours? the devil she is! She bears no resemblance to you, Mike. You are as ill-looking as she is handsome," he said, laughing.

"She is called pretty," said Marshall, who laughed also at the compliment Wing had paid him.

"She is d—d pretty, and resolute too. By Jove! I like her; she is the right sort. We must be better friends before I leave port—and we shall be," Wing muttered, meaningly, to himself.

After a few moments' longer stay they left the tap-room; where he determined ere he left port to be a frequent visitor. The beauty of Marshall's sister had inspired him with a passion fierce and lustful—a passion, the fire of which could only be allayed by the ruin of the beautiful being who had inspired it; and he resolved to be possessor of the one whose charms had so moved him.

"She may be mine! She must be mine! She shall be mine!" was his determined resolve. Every day found him at the tap-room of the Best Bower, and the maid of the tap-room and himself became very good friends; though she often sharply reproved him for the free familiarity of his manner towards her. Often, in the back room, was he found in company with Marshall's sister, in conversation with her.

But there was a watchful eye upon him. Marshall watched over his sister with a deep jealousy. He was fearful of Wing; he suspected him, and watched him sharply.

Wing, hour after hour, in company with the sister of Marshall, sought to beguile and corrupt the heart of the fair, unpolluted girl, with honied words, whispered in warm impassioned tones to her ear. He talked of love—ha, ha! She smiled—a smile of incredulity. Could she read him? Could she see his purpose? Warm and passionate were his words. She smiled. Ardent vows he made of love for her. But those vows were vain—they were unheeded by her. And that cold, incredulous smile that continually wreathed her lips, told him at length that his words and vows, falsely uttered, were uttered in vain—were unheeded—wasted on the air.

He knew that these would not effect his purpose, and he resolved on other means to accomplish the fell purpose of his heart. The smile that wreathed her lips maddened him. The fire of base passion burned within him, and he swore she should be his. In his guilty heart he swore that oath—the ruin of a fair young girl.

He laid a plan, a well contrived plan, to get her into his power, and attempted its execution. But his plan was frustrated, thwarted, by the brother of his meditated victim. Marshall had frustrated the design of the villain, which had well nigh succeeded. By his watchfulness he had saved his sister from the power of a villain—from disgrace.

Wing did not know how his plan had been defeated, nor did Marshall disclose to him his knowledge of it. His sister he placed where she would no more be in danger of the villain, whom he swore to punish at some convenient opportunity, and punish him with a will.

Wing was at a loss to conceive how he had been foiled in his scheme, and he was vexed and maddened to think that his victim was snatched from him when almost within his certain grasp, and by means unknown to him.

He did for a moment half-suspect Marshall; but the latter, not in the least changed to appearance in his manner towards him, lulled his suspicions, and he attributed to accident the failure of his plan. One morning he entered the tap-room of the Best Bower, a week afterwards.

"Well, Marshall, I'm off this morning, rather unexpectedly," he said, as he advanced to Marshall and extended his hand to him, which the latter grasped and shook, as though he shook the hand of his best friend. "I hate to part with you, Mike," said Wing, as he still shook the hand of the other.

"Yes, it is hard for friends to part. I am sorry to part with *you* so *soon*, Wing," said Marshall, in a peculiar tone of emphatic meaning. "So, you sail this morning?"

"Yes; and I go as first, and not second in command of the 'White Cloud.' I am Captain Wing now, Mike."

"Indeed, that's well. But how did you get the berth? Where is Captain Seawood?"

"Oh, he occupies a place six-by-two, or rather, he will soon," said Wing, laughing carelessly.

"Do you mean by that he is dead?"

"Yes, dead as a dead man ever dared to be."

"So you owe the captaincy to his death?"

"Oh, no, it was mine before he died," said Wing, in a careless tone.

"How? explain, Wing."

"Why, you must know that Seawood was a gambler. He had long been a gamester. His passion for gaming was greater than mine, and that was needless. Hardly a day passed during the cruise of the 'White Cloud,' but he and I indulged the passion we both possessed. Sometimes he was the winner, and sometimes myself. It was neck and neck with us. He won, and I lost. I won, and he lost. And thus we alternately lost and won through the whole cruise; and when we arrrived in port, he was no winner, nor I a loser. He had lost a princely fortune by gambling; but this had not cooled his passion. Gaming with him possessed a charm he could not resist. Though a gambler, he was a noble fellow as ever walked dry land, or sailed the sea.

"Yesterday he received from the owners of the brigantine his share of the money that had accrued from the capture we had made. He received two thousand dollars. He flew to the gaming table—to lose it. He pressed me to accompany him, which I did. We played. Fortune, which had so evenly favored us during the cruise, last night wholly deserted him. Fortune favored me. In less time than I've been telling you of it, Mike, I won all the money he possessed; aye, to the last dollar. I would have thrown it back to him, but I knew his proud spirit would have scorned the act; it would have wounded him more, tenfold, than would the loss of the money.

"After he had lost all, he said —'Wing, there is one thing I have left, which I prize more than ten times the amount of money you have won from me. If you will, I will stake it against the amount you have won.'

"'What is that?' I asked.

"'The command of the 'White Cloud,' was his answer.

"That surprised me. I liked it nevertheless.

"'Will you stake that, Captain Seawood?' said I.

"'I will,' he answered firmly.

"We played. As I live I did not exert myself in the game. I wished he might win. But fortune was again in my favor. I won the command of the brigantine. I offered to restore that to him. I could have shot him upon the deck of the brigantine to have obtained her command; but yet, when I had obtained it so easily, I did not like to take it from him. He refused to receive it back. 'No,' said he, 'I would as soon take back the money you have won, as that. You have won it; it is yours; and without another word he left the room. I could not follow him. I pitied him; and, Marshall, never do I remember that my eye was moistened by a tear till last night. But I soon got over it; it was my good fortune, you know. He might have won all I possessed; if he had, why, that would have been his good fortune.

"So I resolved not to let my good fortune cause me any sorrow. Well, what did I hear this morning but the suicide of Captain Seawood—he had blown his brains out. No cause could be assigned for the rash act. None could assign a cause; but I rather think I can. So you see, Marshall, I am Captain of the brigantine, if the owners agree, and of that there is no doubt."

"Poor Seawood! he came to a sad end," said Marshall, as Wing ended.

"But the brigantine will not sail to-day, Wing."

"Well, I guess I was rather fast; I suppose we shall wait till he is under the sod. Has your pretty sister returned yet, Marshall?"

"No; and I shouldn't wonder if she didn't return before you sailed," said Marshall, in a tone that implied he was very confident she would not.

"She has been gone a week; she likes the country life, I guess?"

"Yes;" only answered Marshall.

"Well, she is a pretty girl, and you must look out for her, Marshall," said the hypocritical Wing.

"I intend to. Are you going?"

"Yes, good-bye, Marshall. Remember me to the pretty Nance, if I should not come in again before I sail."

Wing as he spoke departed from the tap-room.

"Yes, yes, I'll remember you to her, *and I shall not forget you, Will Wing, depend upon it.* I can knock his cruise in the head, if I have a mind, by a few words to the owners of the brigantine; but I will let him sail. When he returns, I'll have a reckoning!"

CHAPTER X.

THE PIRACY.

THE second morning after his conversation with Marshall, Wing stood upon the deck of the beautiful brigantine, which was gliding swiftly down the harbour before a smart breeze. He stood proudly upon the deck, the master of the beautiful craft that glided so gallantly over the blue waves.

The command was now his; the one who had held it before him had parted with his life when he parted with the command of the brigantine. But to Wing it mattered not by what means the command had become his. He knew that indirectly he was the cause of Captain Seawood's death; but he cared not, the thought troubled him not. He was now the captain of the privateer; he thought and cared for nothing else.

Swiftly flew the brigantine over the flashing waters, the white sea-foam curling and bubbling around her bows, and lying like a snow-wreath along her sides. Swiftly and lightly she flew over the blue waves, till the receding shores were lost to the eye.

On she sailed, hour after hour, day after day, till she danced over warmer waters—till a warmer sun gilded her snow-white canvass.

For months the privateer "White Cloud" sailed on the Atlantic; but the success that attended her upon her first cruise was not her's the second cruise. Success seemed to have abandoned her; she met with none. Six months she cruised the blue Atlantic, and made not a single capture. There was grumbling and dissatisfaction among the crew. Captain Wing cursed bitterly the ill-luck that attended him, and bitterly cursed the crew, who, discontented with their fruitless cruise, pressed the Captain to return, and swore they would no longer do duty.

Wing refused, and swore he would cruise till the war was ended, nor enter a port, except for water and provisions.

One day there came to him a brawling seaman, who addressed him in a dissatisfied manner.

"Captain Wing, I am sick of this cruise, as are many others aboard. We've cruised six months, and not a capture has been made, and are likely to cruise for six months longer with no better luck. We want to return, and we will!"

With a frown black as night, and his eyes flashing with unrestrained rage, and in a fierce tone, Wing spoke—

"Cease your brawling, lubber. You will not return till I return; and I shall not return till we have made at least one capture; so no more words;" and he ordered the seaman away, and to some duty.

The seaman refused to do his bidding, and his refusal brought his death.

Wing uttered an oath of fierce rage, and drew forth a pistol, exclaiming, in a fierce tone,—

"This is rank mutiny, and this is my reward for mutiny!" and as he spoke he levelled the pistol at the head of the seaman, and fired.

A yell followed the report of the pistol, and the seaman lay on the deck, at the feet of Wing, a corpse.

"Throw him overboard!" said Wing, fiercely, pointing to the bleeding corpse.

His order was obeyed, and quickly.

"Now, if there is another upon the deck who would follow that fellow, let him speak. You are silent now; and keep ye so, if ye value your lives; for I swear I will shoot the first grumbler! You have my oath; remember it! I shall keep it, if ye give me cause."

The Captain spoke in a fierce, determined tone, and as he ended he walked aft. Well knew that crew with whom they had to deal; well knew they that discontent brought death to him who openly expressed it.

"Mardon!" called Wing, as he walked aft, to him who was the first officer of the privateer, "Mardon, here!"

He was in a moment joined by the officer. The two stood aloof from all others, and for some moments were engaged in conversation. It was begun by Wing, in a low tone, who said,—

"Mardon, I intend to run into Havana; we are within six hours' sail of that port, and I mean to run in. We have cruised for six months, and not a prize. Plenty of English men-of-war to run away from, but not an English merchantman have we seen. I am

DEATH OF THE MUTINEER.

sick of this as any on board the brigantine, and I intend to look for other game than Englishmen, for them we cannot find. What think you of the men, Mardon? Suppose we should fall in with a richly laden Don, or any other beside the English flag, would it do to propose—"

The Captain stopped, and looked into the face of the officer with an expression of significant meaning.

"I understand you, Captain Wing," said Mardon, in a moment; "you wish to know if the men would be over-scrupulous in regard to capturing a prize that does not carry English colors?"

"Exactly, Mardon."

"I believe there is a portion of the crew that would not be particular in that respect, Captain Wing," said Mardon, in an under tone.

"Well, Mardon, drop a hint to those you think would make no serious objections, and find how many among the crew we can trust, in case we should fall in with some tempting prey. Put her away now for Havana, Mardon."

The course of the brigantine was altered, and she stood swiftly on, in a direction more westerly. A few hours' sail brought her within sight of the Spanish port, which she was rapidly nearing.

The red sun was rolling down the western arch of the azure sky, and nearly dipped in the ocean, as the brigantine glided over the flashing waters abreast of the Moro Castle.

As she glided past the sullen fortress, the roar of the sunset gun boomed over the waters, which had now lost their robe of fire, as the sun had sunk in its red car of fire in the western ocean, yet leaving the horizon glowing with rich, roseate hues. Long lingered the twilight, as it does in those sunny climes, as if unwilling to yield its glowing beauties to the sombre shades of night.

The brigantine came to anchor as night began to darken the waters of the harbour, and she lay motionless upon the dark water, amidst numerous other craft.

The beauty and matchless symmetry of the brigantine attracted many an eye as she entered the harbour; many an eye was fastened upon her, and many warm exclamations of praise were bestowed upon her by Spanish, French, and English tongues; for men of all these nations, and others, gazed at the American privateer as she proudly entered the harbour, with the gorgeous flag of Spain and the United States waving proudly at her mast-heads.

Three weeks in the harbour of Havana the brigantine lay at anchor, during which time she was visited by hundreds from the town, attracted by her extraordinary beauty. Wing was on shore nearly all the time, as were the crew, who had liberty one half one day, the other half the next.

One night, just three weeks after the privateer had entered she harbour, Wing came on board, having been pulled off to the brigantine by a shore boat. The expression of his face told that something of an unusual nature was passing in his mind.

"Is Mardon on board?" he inquired quickly, as he touched the deck of a seaman nearest him.

"No, he went ashore at noon, and has not returned," was the answer.

"When he comes, tell him I would see him in the cabin."

"Aye, aye, sir," returned the seaman, as Wing walked to the cabin companion-way, down which he disappeared. He entered the splendid cabin, and threw himself upon a couch. For some time he remained in deep thought; when he suddenly started up from his reclining posture, and walked the cabin with rapid paces. His brow was contracted into a heavy frown, and his face betrayed the existence of thoughts of a desperate nature within him. His well chiselled lips were tightly compressed, and an expression of determined resolve rested upon them.

As he walked the cabin to and fro, his eye kindled with the excitement of his thoughts, and flashed and gleamed with a wild fire. Suddenly he exclaimed, almost fiercely—

"By Heaven! I'll do it. I am resolved. It is a fearful barrier to overleap, but I am determined upon it. Ha! Mardon, you have come."

As he spoke, that officer entered the cabin. Wing turned the key in the lock of the cabin door, and then said—

"Well, Mardon, I have something of some importance to disclose to you; but before I say anything further, what of the men? Have you learned who among them are game—how many we can trust?"

"I have, Captain; I know the minds of nearly all the crew, and as I told you when first you mentioned to me your wish, the greater part of the men are not over-scrupulous; we can safely count on eighty out of the ninety."

"Do you think as many, Mardon?" asked Wing, in a sudden manner, as if surprised, and yet pleased.

"I do, Captain Wing," said the officer, in a confident tone.

"That will do well," said Wing, in an elated tone "If eighty out of the ninety are game, the others we can *silence*, you know, Mardon."

He spoke in a significant manner, and his meaning was well understood by his officer.

"Well, Mardon, I suppose you are—"

"I am with you, Captain Wing," said the officer, breaking in upon the Captain, as if he divined what he would have said.

"We are one, then; and I will now make known to you what I have learned—something we may now consider important. You have seen the Spanish ship that lies moored between us and the town, the 'Isabella?'

"Yes, and she is a fine ship, to look at, and they

say, a capital sailor," said Mardon. "But what of her, Captain?"

"Well, she sails the day after to-morrow."

"Ay, and she goes out to old Spain, richly laden. A Spanish nobleman sails in her, and carries immense wealth."

"Mardon, in my own mind I have resolved to fall in with the 'Isabella,' and lighten her of a portion of the wealth she carries. What say you?"

"I am yours, heart and hand, Captain Wing," said Mardon, with animation in his tone. "If we succeed, it will be *privateering* to some profit, Captain," he again said, laughing.

"*If* we succeed? by ——! if I attempt it, I will not fail," said Wing, in a tone of fierce determination. "I swear if I attempt it, Mardon, the wealth the 'Isabella' carries shall be mine. If I fail, I'll blow the brigantine to the four winds of Heaven!"

The words of the privateer captain were spoken in a tone of stern, determined resolve, and sealed with an oath.

"What is her crew, Captain?"

"Twenty-five men, and carries four guns," said Wing. "Mardon, shall we do this? shall we have the 'Isabella's' wealth? or shall we let it slip through our fingers, when we can obtain possession of it so easily?"

Wing folded his arms across his breast, and gazed into the face of his officer, as if yet with some anxiety as to his answer. But a moment, and Mardon answered—

"I am for the undertaking, Captain. It is a prize we should not lose."

"We will have it, then," said Wing, in a tone quick and determined. "The 'Isabella' shall be ours. She sails the day after to-morrow; we must sail to-morrow, and lay off and on and watch for her, and attack her in the night. By sailing to-morrow, there will be no suspicion, if at all, of the brigantine being the pirate. I will now return on shore; you can pop the affair to those whom you think are with us, that they may not be in ignorance as to the object of our sailing. Let not another man leave the brigantine while she lays here. I shall be on board by ten o'clock in the morning, and then the brigantine weighs anchor."

Unlocking the cabin door as he spoke, the Captain departed. The night passed, the morn broke, the red sun rose, and mounting the azure heavens, poured down his golden rays, suffusing earth and ocean with his golden effulgence. It was near the hour of ten; the hour Wing had fixed to be on board. He had not yet come, and Mardon stood upon the quarter-deck of the brigantine watching for his appearance anxiously. He at length discovered a boat making towards the brigantine, which contained the Captain. The boat soon touched alongside, and Wing in a moment stood on the deck.

"Shall we get ready for sea, Captain?" asked Mardon.

"Yes, get the brigantine under weigh immediately," was the prompt reply of Wing.

"Loose the topsails and jib, and heave the anchor up!" shouted Mardon.

In an instant the rigging held a score of men, climbing aloft to execute the command of the officer. The anchor hove a-peak, the brigantine began to move slowly over the gently undulating waves. Gradually her motion through the water became accelerated. The surging of the water around her bows, and the gurgling under the counter was heard as she cut through the flashing waves.

A little while and she was abreast of the Moro Castle. As she passed the sullen fortress, a gun was fired from the deck, a parting salute, which was returned from the castle, and the brigantine passed swiftly on, now under a press of sail, her canvass swelling out like balloons from her towering masts.

On danced the gallant craft proudly over the sunlit waves. On she glided, leaving the sunny isle rapidly astern, till the towers and battlements of the Moro Castle faded in the distance. Wing was walking in thoughtful mood the blood-red deck of the brigantine. Half-an-hour he paced the deck fore and aft, in communion with the dark thoughts that crowded his brain, when he approached Mardon, who stood leaning against the bulwarks on the starboard bow.

"Mardon," he said, in a low tone, "have you mentioned to the trusty ones of the crew our intention?"

"I have, Captain," answered the officer.

"How did they take it?

"Heartily; with a will. You made a good selection of your crew in Boston, captain. Eighty out of the ninety will make as good freebooters as ever sailed, or robbed a ship. But, captain, do you ever intend to return to Boston?"

"I do, most certainly," answered Wing; and as he spoke, a settled and meaning expression rested upon his face. "There is a pretty bird there, Mardon, that I must cage; and when I have caged her, we'll fly from Boston together, never to return again."

"A woman, captain, I suppose you mean?" said Mardon, smiling.

"Yes, as pretty a woman as ever your two eyes beheld. When I leave Boston again, she goes with me."

"Voluntarily?" said Mardon, inquiringly.

"I rather think not. But stolen fruit is the sweetest, they say, Mardon," said Wing, with a leer in his eye.

"It is. But you calculate rather too surely upon returning to Boston, Captain. Unless you run for that port as soon as the ship is attended to, the affair will be known all over the United States. The brigantine will be known by those on board the

'Isabella,' and unless we silence every one on board of her, she will return to port, and we are done for."

"I have thought of that before now, Mardon. No fear. The 'Isabella' will be eased of a portion of her wealth, and none on board of her shall be the wiser as to who were the plunderers."

"How mean you, Captain Wing?" said Mardon, with surprise in his tones.

"As I have said," answered Wing, "that those on board the 'Isabella' will never know who robbed the ship; that is, in case a plan of mine succeeds. I shall know whether to board the ship or not, by a signal, before those on board of her can make out the brigantine."

"A signal! Have you friends aboard the ship, Captain?" asked Mardon, surprised at the words of Wing.

"One," answered Wing; "but I'll tell you more about this after the affair is over. I am all impatience for to-morrow night. May the hours speed on as swiftly as the brigantine speeds over the waves, is my wish!"

Swiftly was the "White Cloud" borne over the flashing waters; swiftly did she cleave through the wave-crests of the sea; lightly she danced over her native element, till the night donned its dark mantle, and cast o'er the ocean its gloomy pall. Wing paced the deck, cursing the hours that seemed to his impatient spirit to pass so slowly. As the middle watch was set, he ordered the officer of the watch to tack ship and stand for the island, and then went below.

The morn broke, and the brigantine stood on for the Isle of Cuba till noon, when the faint outline of the island appeared on the distant verge of the blue horizon. As the isle became visible, Wing again gave orders to tack, and stand away. A short time, and the dim outline of the isle now astern faded from the sight, and the brigantine stood away till night again closed in, when she again tacked and stood once more for the island. As the first watch was set, Wing, who stood upon the forecastle, called to Mardon, who joined him on the instant.

"Send two of our trustiest men aloft, Mardon, to keep a sharp look-out for the ship; they must keep a sharp look-out ahead for her, for we must not get too near before I have the signal. Go!"

Mardon left him to do his bidding, and the two look-outs were in a few moments sent aloft, and the officer returned to where Wing stood, his gaze bent ahead.

CHAPTER XI.

THE TORNADO.

IT was a lovely night. The clear blue heavens, studded with myriads of stars, seemed like an arching canopy of azure suspended over the deep blue of the ocean, inlaid with countless glittering gems of brightest lustre.

"What is the signal you expect, Captain?" asked Mardon, as he approached Wing.

"A blue light. It will be burned, if things work right, as soon as the brigantine can be made out."

Anxiously did Wing watch with his night glass for the appearance of the Spanish ship. His mind was so resolved upon the piracy, that the thought of missing his object rendered him extremely impatient, and he cursed immoderately at the thought of missing the expected prize.

Anxiously he swept the dark ocean around, with his night glass, till the ringing of "eight bells" sounded on the night, breaking the stillness with the musical tones. It was now the midnight hour. For a few moments all was bustle on the deck of the brigantine, by the changing of the watch, but the first watch relieved, all was silent in a few moments.

Wing stood with his night glass yet to his eye, sweeping the dark ocean, and giving vent to the impatience that pressed him, by the frequent utterance of oaths.

"D——n! shall I miss what my whole mind has dwelt on so many hours in anticipation?" he exclaimed to himself in a fierce, impatient tone. "Ha! there is a sail on our starboard bow!" he suddenly exclaimed a moment after. "May the fiends grant it is the 'Isabella!'

Hardly had the words left his lips, when simultaneously the cry of "Sail, ho!" came from the two look-outs aloft.

"Where away?" quickly demanded Wing.

"About three points on our starboard bow," was the answer from one.

"That's it!" said Wing; and he sprang into the starboard forerigging, and levelled his glass in the direction the sail had been discovered. For a number of minutes he stood with his gaze bent intently upon the sail that loomed darkly up in the distance.

"What do you make her out, Captain?" asked Mardon, impatient to know what the sail was.

"A ship—it must be the 'Isabella!'" returned Wing, in a tone elated and confident.

"Pipe all hands on deck!—take in the light sails, and haul up the courses, Mardon. I don't want to get too near, if it should be her."

In a few minutes the men were all on deck, and

the order of Wing was quickly executed, and the brigantine now moved slowly through the water, under her fore-topsail and mainsail.

An hour passed, during which time Wing had watched with the utmost impatience for the expected signal.

The ship, bearing directly down for the brigantine, now loomed up so as to be visible without the aid of a glass.

Wing kept his eyes bent upon her with the deepest impatience, which he betrayed by his frequent oaths. Anxiously he awaited the signal from the ship; the moments seemed hours to him.

"He must have made out the brigantine ere now," he said, in a tone that betrayed somewhat of doubt. "He has, Mardon; there is the signal!" he exclaimed, in the same breath, in a tone quick and excited.

At the very instant, the ocean was illuminated by a bright blue light, which revealed for an instant the stately ship in the distance with perfect distinctness. A moment more, and all was darkness again upon the ocean.

"Lower away the boats, and man them," cried Wing, a moment after the signal light.

The three boats which the brigantine carried were soon alongside and manned.

"Let fall and pull away for the ship," said Wing, as he seated himself in the stern-sheets of the cutter.

The three boats dashed away from the brigantine, which now lay motionless upon the water with her fore-topsail aback.

Swiftly dashed the boats over the waves toward the stately ship looming up a-head, and which was approaching toward them rapidly.

In ten minutes the ship was in hailing distance.

"We can't board the ship going at this rate, Captain," said Mardon, breaking the silence.

"We must though, if we board her at all!" said Wing. "Hold on, men," he said; at the same moment the men ceased pulling at the oars, and the boat was put about.

In two minutes the ship was within fifty feet of the cutter, which lay rocking upon the waves right abeam.

"Let fall and give away now," said Wing; and the boat leaped through the water toward the ship, and in a few seconds was dashing alongside, within a few feet of her, in a parallel course.

"Throw me the rope," shouted Wing, as the boat shot close under the starboard gangway.

"Ay, ay!" was returned by some one on board the ship, and at the same time a rope was thrown over the side.

The boat was hauled close alongside, and Wing, and the rest in the cutter, ascended the ship's side by means of the gangway ladder.

"Back the fore-topsail," said Wing, the moment his men touched the deck, in order to bring the ship to.

In a moment the foreyard of the ship swung aback to the mast, and in a short time she lay motionless upon the water. The other two boats now came alongside, and were made fast, and their crews ascended to the deck of the ship.

Mardon and the others, who knew nothing of the plan of Wing, stood upon the deck in speechless wonder at what they beheld. The crew of the Spanish ship lay here and there upon the deck, as if asleep or dead. None of the ship's crew were encountered by the crew of the brigantine, save one, who was conversing with Wing; all lay motionless upon the deck. A strange sight, and to the brigantine's crew, unaccountable.

"Are they all asleep, Gomez?" was the first question Wing asked the Spaniard.

"All," returned the latter.

"The Captain?"

"Yes."

"The potion worked well. You dosed them all, Gomez?"

"Yes," said the Spaniard.

"Well, now for the gold. The doubloons, Gomez, where are they?"

The Spaniard turned and walked aft, motioning Wing to follow, and both descended into the cabin. The Spaniard lifted a small trap in the after part of the cabin, and took therefrom two bags, and then let fall the trap.

"Is that all?" demanded Wing, as the Spaniard laid the two bags of gold at his feet.

"Yes," answered the latter.

"But where is the Don's gold?"

"He did not sail with us. He is in Havana, and has his gold with him," said the Spaniard.

"D——n!" ejaculated Wing, in a fierce tone of disappointment. "We have lost that. How much is there here, Gomez?"

"One thousand doubloons."

"Sixteen thousand dollars. Well, bring the bags on deck, we'll be sure of them;" and as he spoke, Wing left the cabin, followed by the Spaniard with the bags of gold.

As he gained the deck he ordered the men into the boats, after having squared the fore yards of the ship. He and the Spaniard followed immediately.

The stately ship began to move through the water, as the cutter was cast free from her, and in a few moments was under full headway, her crew lying upon her deck unconscious of the visit that had been paid them. The three boats dashed on toward the brigantine, the cutter ahead with its freight of gold.

"We shall have a blow before long, I'm thinking," observed Wing, casting a look to sky-ward, as the cutter dashed away from the ship. "It's black as pitch overhead."

A sudden change of the weather had come on. The sky, but a few moments before so clear and bright, was now overcast with black and threatening clouds. Each moment they grew darker and more wild. A fierce tornado was in those black and frowning clouds, and threatening momentarily to leap forth, and lash the ocean into foam with its angry breath.

Impenetrable darkness now settled upon the ocean, succeeded by a fearful stillness. The wind died suddenly away, and the waves sank in seeming repose into the bosom of the deep. Suddenly came from the far off south a low moaning sound, gradually increasing to a heavy rumbling like far distant thunder.

"Give way, men! give way, lively!" cried Wing, who was aware the tornado, yet chained in the clouds, would ere long burst in all its fury upon the ocean. All were aware of the threatening danger, and bent to their pliant oars with redoubled vigor. The boats seemed to leap from the now calm water, so swiftly they dashed onward. Nearer, louder, and fiercer grew that moaning of the winds.

"Good God! Mardon, look astern!" exclaimed Wing, in a vehement tone. "We shall have that wall of foam upon us before we can reach the brigantine," he said, in a tone that betrayed fearful anxiety.

On the near horizon could be seen a dazzling line of white sea foam, driven madly forward by the tornado.

"Give way, men, for your lives! give way, or we are lost!" again exclaimed Wing, in a voice that betrayed his fears for the safety of the boats.

Louder and fiercer roared the winds, and the ocean was lashed into billows of foam. Every soul was struck with dread at the fearful sound.

Swiftly leaped the boats over the foaming billows for a few seconds longer, when the brigantine was dimly made out in the darkness, about twice the length of the cutter ahead.

"There she is; one more pull, my men, and we are alongside," said Wing, in a lively tone, relieved of fear.

"Ho, the quarter-boats!" he shouted at the top of his voice, for they could not be seen in the darkness.

"Ho, the cutter!" was returned in a moment from the boats.

"They are safe, and right upon us; one more pull, men."

Almost as he spoke the three boats touched the brigantine alongside, and their crews were quickly upon her deck.

The boats were quickly hoisted in, and the brigantine was put square before the fierce hurricane, under her fore-topsail close-reefed.

It was but a moment ere that white and glaring wall of foam was upon her. It leaped madly over her taffrail, as if to overwhelm her. For a moment the brigantine was submerged to her gunwales in the wild whirlpool of waters, and struggled like a thing of life to free herself from the heavy weight that bore her down. At length she emerged from the wild vortex of waters, and rode proudly and gallantly on the billowy sea, driven on by the fierce hurricane with a fearful velocity.

But the ship; how rides she before the fearful blast? With every sail spread broad to the gale, with no human hand to guide her, left entirely to the guidance of the fierce winds and waves, she dashed madly on before the raging tornado, the angry waves tossing the noble structure in their mighty strength like a feather; now bearing her to their towering crests, and now sinking her in their fearful hollows, down, down, as if to bury her for ever.

On she drove, on, on the billows of boiling foam; on, with the fierce tornado driving her with fearful velocity forward to destruction. On, with her every sail spread to the fierce gale, she drove; while on her foam-washed deck lay her crew in a death-like stupor, unconscious of the wild tempest around: death-like they lay, unconscious of their threatened doom. On drove the noble ship over the maddened sea, bearing her unconscious crew to their doom.

O God! will they not rouse up from their death-like stupor, and save themselves and the noble vessel that bears them from the doom that threatens them? No, they cannot; they lay chained upon the wave-washed deck in their unconsciousness. And unconscious will they meet their doom—a fearful one. It was the foulest work of hell that laid them there; and fearfully must he atone, who was the instrument in this foul work.

For half-an-hour was the ship driven on wholly at the mercy of the wild hurricane, and cloud-tossed angry waves—half-an-hour, and yet her crew lay death-like upon her decks.

Louder and louder, and wilder grew the wrath of the tornado; and wilder roared and higher tossed the maddened billows. And onward drove the ship in her mad career; now leaping to the crest of a high towering wave, now plunging in the deep hollow of the foaming sea.

Nobly did she cope with and withstand the fury of the wild tossing billows, and still wilder winds; struggling like a living thing, as it seemed, with the strength of despair, for life in an unequal contest.

Suddenly the wind veered round to the northward, and for a single instant lulled away. It was but an instant, and then the fierce blast from the north burst upon the ocean, and came sweeping on with tenfold fury.

The fierce blast struck the ship as she rode on the foaming crest of the towering wave: every sail was taken aback, and in an instant the stately ship that had rode the gale triumphantly till now, was borne over by the furious blast on her beam-ends, as she sunk with the wave in the hollow of the sea; and her canvass was ripped from her yards by the waves in their fury.

An instant, and she was caught and borne on the breast of a mountain billow to its foaming crest, that reared itself almost to the near hurricane clouds above, and for a moment was poised on the foam-crest of the cloud-reared billow.

Then down with the wave she sank; down, into the deep, deep, trough of boiling foam, she sank. Down, with the wild whirlwind upon her; down, beneath the wild whirlpool of waters, she sank to rise no more. The raging billow closed over the doomed ship and her doomed crew for ever.

But how suddenly has the elemental strife ceased! That last fearful blast from the north was the last breath of the expiring gale. The mad fury of the dread tornado was spent. It had died away more suddenly than it had burst upon the ocean. Had the ship lived through that last short-lived but fiercest blast, she would now have rode the waves in triumph and safety.

The frowning clouds that curtained the heavens now parted; and here and there became visible a glittering star, which shone with unwonted lustre. The waves that had raged so wildly began to subside; and the white foam that had robed the bosom of the angry deep was changing to its usual color.

CHAPTER XII.

THE MURDER.

THE gallant brigantine had rode bravely out the gale in safety, and was now under the controul of her helm, and able to carry sail. The wind had again changed, and now blew moderately from the south.

"The storm is over, and the brigantine has proved herself a gallant craft," said Wing to his lieutenant, as they stood upon the quarter-deck.

"Yes, she rode it out fine; but the ship must have gone—"

"To the devil!" said Wing, while a laugh rang from his lips. "That blast from the north must have struck her all aback, and she must have gone down by the stern, with all her crew."

"I would like to know, Captain Wing, of the plan you conceived for robbing the ship. I can't account for the men lying about the deck as if dead. If you please, inform me."

"Oh, certainly, Mardon. You will very easily account for that, when you know how. This Spaniard, Gomez, was the steward of the ship. I fell in with him in Havana, and made friends with him. He was a very communicative fellow: I learned from him when the ship was to sail, and that she carried out a considerable amount of gold, which we have safely aboard. He also informed me that a Spanish nobleman was to take passage to old Spain, with well-filled trunks. To my great disappointment, Mardon, the wealthy Don remained in Havana, and saved his gold. Well, I proposed, in a joking manner, to capture the ship; told this Gomez I should do it. He said to me, in a tone and manner that surprised me, that I could not do it with my vessel (he knew the brigantine), for it would soon be known all over the States that an American privateer had committed piracy. I said to him I was only joking. To my great surprise, he said to me, that he could so contrive it, that I could take the gold from the ship the night after she sailed, without its ever being known who were the authors of the piracy. I asked him how it could be done? and he said I should know if I would allow him half the spoils. I promised this, and urged him to tell me how it was to be done. He then said he could obtain a drug, that if taken in any drink, would stupify for hours the one who took it. He said he could easily stretch the whole crew in a stupor like death, in which they would remain for hours by means of this drug. I asked him if he would do this, and he said if I was agreed he would. Wasn't he a jewel, Mardon? Well, we agreed upon it; he was to drug the crew the night after the ship sailed, I was to board her and get the gold, and he was to have one half and leave the ship. How well he succeeded in doing his part of the plot, you already know."

"Do you intend to give him half of this gold, Captain?" asked Mardon, in a manner rather sudden.

"That was the bargain," answered Wing. "If I should break it, he might grumble, you know."

"Let him grumble, and take it out in grumbling. Give him eight thousand dollars!—I would see him in the devil's kingdom first! Get him out of the way—pitch him overboard accidentally!"

"Well, Mardon, to tell the truth, I did not mean to keep the bargain. He'll have none of the gold: I have it safely in the cabin."

"Well, it is best to get rid of him; he may give us a dose of his medicine. I have no disposition to try its virtue myself."

"He may, though; I did not think of that. But I'll attend to him. We will divide the gold among the men. Give the eighty, if there is as many who will take it, ten doubloons a-piece; we shall have two hundred between us. What say you to that?"

"I leave all that to you. Do as you like. But how shall we manage those who refuse to take the gold, as countenancing the manner in which we obtained it?"

"If they won't take the gold, make them swear to keep the secret, or die. The oath or death! One or the other they must choose."

"They will take the oath, probably, and break it as soon as they get on shore, if we run into any port."

"But I will take care they don't leave the vessel, Mardon, when she returns to port. I mean to return to Boston, but do not mean to lay in port twenty-four hours; at least, no longer than I can get on board a pretty maid I know of. If the eighty agree to sail under a flag of our own, when I leave and am off the port, I'll set the others afloat in a boat. They may then make their way back to port, and 'peach, or keep silent, I care not which. There will be nothing known of this affair, except it is betrayed by some of the crew; for the ship must have foundered in this storm, and gone down with all the crew. As to our crew, we must look out for them, that is all. If we are betrayed, we are fools."

The conversation between Wing and his officer now ceased, and they went below, just as the helmsman sung out "Eight bells!"

The strokes of the by-gone watch were tolled upon the brigantine's bell, by the boatswain's mate, and the watch was again changed.

The next morn broke bright and beautiful upon the ocean, and the brigantine was dancing gaily over the dark waters of the Mexican Gulf. It was near ten o'clock, when Wing came on deck. After a short conversation with his lieutenant, he spoke to the crew, telling them that the gold that had been taken from the ship would be divided among those that would accept it and keep the secret of its acquisition while in any port the brigantine should make.

"All who swear to keep this secret, will range on the starboard deck," he now said.

All but ten stood upon the starboard side of the deck.

"And what do you intend to do?" asked Wing of the ten who kept the larboard side.

"We do not intend to take that oath!" answered a young seaman, in a bold, undaunted tone. "The first port the brigantine enters, I will make known this piracy, if I but get on shore!"

"And do you think I would let you leave the vessel without the oath?" said Wing, with a sagacious smile on his lips. "No, no, if you wo'n't of your own will keep the secret, we will compel you to keep it. You shall not leave the vessel when she enters a port, without taking the oath."

"And that we will not do!" said the young sailor, boldly

"As you like. Nay, by Heaven, you shall swear the oath, or you will keep the secret safer yet!" said Wing, in a tone of determined and significant meaning.

"We refuse!" said the young seaman, in a spirited tone.

"Your refusal is your death-warrant, then! The oath or death! I give you five minutes to decide the choice."

The half-score of seamen stood huddled together in conversation, till Wing, who had kept his eye upon his watch, remarked that the five minutes were up.

"We had best take the oath," said the young man who had been the spokesman for the ten, in an under tone, as Wing called out. "By so doing we shall escape the death this pirate will surely award us, and some day or other bring him to a just punishment. If we take the oath, we shall be allowed to go ashore when the brigantine enters port. Ashore, I shall no longer consider the oath binding, but shall make known this piracy."

"The time is up, I say!" said Wing again, in a stern tone.

"We take the oath!" said the seaman immediately.

"I believed you would; death is no welcome choice. You swear?"

"We do!"

"Enough. You have well and easily avoided death. Mardon!" he called to his first officer; "go down and bring up the gold. We will divide it now. Cut the bags open upon the deck, and distribute it as I mention," he said, as Mardon appeared with the two bags.

The gold was counted and distributed, ten doubloons each to eighty of the crew, and the same amount offered to the other ten, but they refused it.

While this was being done, Gomez, the Spaniard, came up to Wing and said, in a surly tone, and his brow darkening—

"I was to have half of this gold you are dividing."

"You was, eh? Was that the bargain though? Really, I did not think of you!"

Wing uttered this in a cool, careless, aggravating tone, that raised the ire of the Spaniard. "My dear fellow, the gold is divided now; you are too late. I am sorry, really! But take ten doubloons, as the rest will.'

The face of the Spaniard became black with rage, at the cool indifference and insulting manner of Wing, and he demanded in a fierce tone the five hundred doubloons.

"Ten is all I can accommodate you with," said Wing coolly, and with a look of indifference.

"I want the five hundred or none!" said the Spaniard, sullenly.

"Your wants can't be complied with," said Wing firmly. "You can have ten or none."

THE ABDUCTION OF GEORGIANA ON HER WEDDING-DAY.

"You have broken this bargain : by all the saints ! you shall never make or break another."

The Spaniard spoke these words with a fierce utterance, and sprang upon Wing, bearing him down upon the deck, his left hand fixed on his throat with an iron-like gripe. In an instant, his raised right hand held a glittering poniard above the breast of Wing, whose face was blackening from suffocation. The dark eyes of the Spaniard shot forth revengeful fire. He poised the glittering steel for an instant for the blow. The steel descended the same moment that a pistol-ball lodged in his brain.

The poniard touched the breast of Wing without harm, and the Spaniard fell back a lifeless corse.

CHAPTER XIII.

THE LOVERS.

NOW, dear reader, with us to the country seat of an opulent and retired merchant, on the banks of the noble, picturesque Hudson, a few miles above its mouth.

It was an elegant mansion, facing the river, with a very extensive and most beautifully laid out garden in front, that reached to the river's bank, along which, like a border, ran a milk-white gravelled walk. This splendid garden was tastefully laid out in squares, circles, diamonds, stars, and crescents; embracing every variety of flowers, and presenting a gorgeous array of colors to the delighted eye, which would never weary gazing at the flowery scene.

Walks of white gravel interspersed the garden, and one broader than the others extended from the walk on the river's bank to the mansion, and was lined on either side its entire length by a row of stately elms, thus forming a delightfully shaded avenue.

The mansion was three stories in height, each story furnished in front with a piazza. A cupola graced the roof, from which could be obtained a splendid panoramic view of the surrounding country, and of the distant bay of New York. The "Highland Home," as the mansion was called, was the property of a Mr. Wheelock, for years a merchant of New York, but now retired, and enjoying his wealth, the fruits of many years of business toil. Here in the summer months he dwelt with a loved and only daughter, a beauteous being whom he loved almost to idolization.

Here in his "Highland Home" lived Colonel Wheelock, contented and truly happy with his lovely and much-loved daughter. The happiness of his daughter was foremost in his mind; it seemed the sole object of his heart, his whole study, to render her happy. She was happy; and in her happiness Colonel Wheelock was most happy. He was about fifty years of age—a portly, noble-looking gentleman, whose face, pleasing to the beholder, was expressive of a warm, generous nature. His was a face that struck the beholder with admiration—once seen, ever to be remembered; a face in which no selfishness of mind was betrayed, but open, frank cordiality, and warm, noble generosity were written there as clearly as the sunlight of Heaven. In every sense of the term Colonel Wheelock was a gentleman; one of the noblest of nature's noblemen. He enjoyed well his wealth. In luxury and splendor he lived, and happily, with his beauteous daughter Georgiana.

In this beautiful mansion, on the banks of the noble Hudson, we would have the reader imagine himself, on a mild afternoon about three months subsequent to the scenes detailed in the foregoing chapter.

Seated by an open casement, robed in simple white, was a young and beautiful maiden. Beautiful was her face, beautiful beyond compare; though a pensive, melancholy look, not habitual, now overspread it. Though her look was melancholy, it robbed no beauty from the face of the maiden, but rendered it supremely lovely.

Gazing listlessly down the broad and lengthy avenue of elms, a rounded, beautifully moulded arm, of alabaster whiteness, resting upon the casement, her dark hair unconfined, falling in clustering ringlets to her neck, fairer than Parian marble; with no jewels adorning her lovely person, save a ring that circled her nuptial finger, set with a surpassingly-brilliant diamond, robed in pure and simple white, sat the beautiful maid of the Highland Home, Georgiana Wheelock.

For an hour she had sat at the open casement in a pensive trance, when suddenly the rapid clattering of a horse's hoofs fell on her ear. She started from her seat, and stood at the casement, gazing with an eager and expectant look down the lengthy avenue before her.

Her glorious dark eyes brightened, and her full lips, that mocked the hue of the reddest rose, were for an instant wreathed with a bright smile. It lingered for an instant upon her ruby lips, like a ray of the sun upon the opening rosebud, then vanished. Her dark eyes, that had lighted up so suddenly with momentary fire, became languid again, and her face of unrivalled beauty wore a look sadder than before; sad, yet beautiful.

The sound that had reached her ear from a distance, each moment grew nearer and nearer, and in a few moments a horseman turned into the avenue of elms from the river's bank, and came toward the mansion at a dashing pace. He was a young man of elegant appearance, and rode his high-mettled steed with a rare grace.

"Good afternoon, Georgie," he said, in a happy tone, as he came up within speaking distance; and lifting his hat, he bowed gracefully to the maiden.

"Good afternoon, dear Howard," returned the maiden, in a half happy, half sad voice, and as she spoke she left the casement, and in a moment stood upon the marble steps of the mansion.

The rider had dismounted from his steed, and fastened the noble, high-blooded "chesnut" to a tree, and now came forward to the beauteous maiden, and taking her fair, small hand within his, with a respectful air, bestowed upon it a kiss.

"Dear Georgie, you are sad," he said, in a tone affectionate and full of sympathy, as he gazed into the face of the fair being before him.

"Do I look sad, dear Howard?" returned the maiden, with a bland smile wreathing her pretty lips.

"In truth you do, dear Georgie; and I shall be sad if you do not smile away this melancholy that is not wont to cloud the beauty of thy face. You smile, and yet there is a sadness dwelling in that smile. Tell me, dearest Georgie! what makes thee melancholy. Nay, dear girl! turn not away from my fond gaze; but tell me why this desponding—why this gloom that clouds thy fair brow? It has changed the radiant smiles that are wont to wreath thy ruby lips, to looks of sorrow; like the dark cloud that shrouds in gloom the fair, bright sunlight of Heaven. Come, dearest Georgie! cheer up, and let the gladsome smiles enliven thy lovely face, and change the gloom into sunshine; ay, and make me happy, for I am not happy when you are sad. Can it be that the heart of Georgiana Wheelock knows a grief? If it is so, unfold to me, dear girl! the cause of that grief. Keep it not from me, but tell me all, all that makes thee unhappy. Dearest Georgie! tell me, I beseech you!—perhaps I have caused thee this unseeming sadness—offended thee in some way unknown to me; tell me, have I —— ?"

"Oh, no, dearest Howard! you never caused me slightest thought of sorrow," said the maiden, in a tone quivering with emotion.

"Nor would I, dearest, knowingly cause a shadow of sadness to rest on thy face. But you will tell me what makes thee unhappy? Who more fitting to know thy grief than myself, dear girl? Let us go to the arbor; you will there unfold to me the cause of thy sadness, will you not, dear girl? Come, you will go."

"Yes, dear Howard!" answered the maiden, and she placed her fair white arm of rounded beauty within his; and the fond lovers walked slowly down the shaded avenue for a short distance, when they turned into a narrow walk that led to a beautiful bower. They were a lovely couple as the eye could wish to see. Her's was a faultless form of beauty, gifted with a graceful carriage. Grace was in her every motion, as she walked lightly by the side of her lover. At every step, a small and handsome foot, encased in a slipper of white satin, peeped out from beneath the folds of the spotless robe of white, and pressed lightly upon the whitened walk—lightly as if disdaining to press its form of provoking beauty to the ground beneath.

The maiden's lover was tall, rather slight, but of elegant form; his carriage easy and graceful, his step firm and elastic. His face was handsome, and deeply expressive; his features bold and beautiful. His brilliant, dark eyes, were full of affection and tenderest devotion, as they rested upon the beauteous being at his side in admiring gaze. In silence the lovers walked slowly towards the bower.

"Now, dearest Georgie, you will tell me what weighs upon thee and makes thee sad," said the young man, in a tone of gentle yet earnest persuasion, as they entered the arbour and seated themselves upon a couch. He encircled his arm around her tapering waist, and drew her willingly to his bosom in warm embrace, and upon her red ripe lips he bestowed a fervent kiss of love. Entwining her beautifully moulded arms of marble whiteness around the neck of her lover, and while her dark, lustrous, soul-expressive eyes, beaming with love, were fixed upon his handsome face, the lovely maiden returned the burning kiss of love, and seemed to have forgotten her sadness in that moment of delicious happiness—happiness such as lovers only know. All was forgotten in that chaste embrace; all, everything but each other. He had no thought but of the beauteous maiden; she had not a thought but of him, her devoted lover. Impatient to know the cause of the beautiful maiden's sadness, her lover was the first to break the happy silence.

"Georgie, dearest," he said fondly, "tell me why this look of melancholy rests on thy fair face? Tell me why you look sad, who never looked sad before?"

"Dear, dear Howard! I am so happy now, that I dread to talk of that which makes me sad," said the beauteous being, fixing her dark, soul-expressive eyes upon the face of her lover, with a look of fondest affection.

"I am most unhappy to know there is aught to make thee sad, dear girl! Come, let me know what causes this sadness, and be sad no more."

The young man spoke in a tone of fond entreaty, and imprinted a kiss upon the marble-like brow of the maiden.

"I will tell you all, dear Howard! all that makes me sad. You have often heard me tell you what my father has often said to me, pleasantly and unmeaningly as I thought, of his intention to wed me to his much loved and intimate friend, Mr. Wing?"

"I have, dear Georgie! and have heard him say the same myself, in a light and pleasant manner. Surely he had no such meaning, dear girl?" said the lover, in an apprehensive voice.

"Many are the times he has said to me, playfully, that I should wed his friend; and as often have I said in return, 'I should be proud to be the wife of his friend.' I spoke thoughtlessly, and as playfully as I supposed he had spoken. I never gave another thought to his words, until he would at some other time repeat them. Imagine my utter surprise, when yesterday morning father asked me whether I had given any thought to what he had often said concerning my union with his friend. His manner was earnest. I replied 'No,' laughing as I spoke. He then said he had thought seriously of it for months, though when he had named it to me it was in a playful manner. Years ago, when my father was engaged in business, he became involved by the failures of several extensive mercantile houses with whom he was in dealing, and who were indebted to him in large amounts. His losses by these houses were so great, that he became insolvent. Ruin threatened him inevitably. He saw that he must become a bankrupt. To an honorable man, the thoughts of bankruptcy crush his soul with despair—it is the bitterest hour of his life. In this most trying hour to my father, there stepped forth a ready friend—a friend indeed, who relieved him from his great embarrassments—saved him from the staring ruin.

That friend was Mr. Wing. During the after years of my father's business-life, Fortune favored him with lavish smiles. He amassed immense wealth; and retired from the merchant's life to live free from its cares and toils. I need not say that from that dark hour of my father's life, until now, that two more ardent, sincere friends, than himself and Mr. Wing, never existed. From my father I learned that Mr. Wing had formed for me an ardent attachment; and that he had acquainted my father of it; had often expressed to him his love for me; and had asked of him my hand in marriage. My father told me this—surprising me. I know that my father would well like to bestow his daughter's hand upon his friend; that he would feel most happy in doing so, provided I would but willingly consent, and feel myself happy in consenting to the marriage. Consent I could, but not be happy.

"Dear Howard, in few words, my father wishes me to marry his friend. He talked long and earnestly with me respecting the union. He told me it would be the happiest moment of his life to see me the wife of his noble friend, if I could be but happy in giving my hand to him. He talked earnestly of his valued friend who had singly aided him, and saved him from the threatened abyss of ruin; and in return for that act of friendship, it would be the happiest moment of his existence to wed me to him. This morn he again spoke further upon the subject for two hours; and asked me if I could not think favorably of what would be the consummation of his most earnest desire. He told me to give thought to it, and to-night let him know my thoughts."

"And is this Colonel Wheelock? Would he thus sacrifice his daughter's happiness by wedding her to a man she cannot love? Can this be your father, who has ever sought to make his daughter the happiest of the happy?"

The maiden's lover spoke in a voice of surprise, and in a tone that cast severe reproof upon her father.

"He would not see his daughter unhappy for an instant, dear Howard," said the maiden, in a gentler tone, and affected almost to tears. "He wishes this union could take place, but he wishes me happy in the union; he would not have me unwillingly wed."

"Then why are you sad, Georgiana? You have but to tell him you cannot consent to this union willingly, and with happiness to yourself."

"I am sad, dear Howard, because I cannot answer him as his heart most earnestly desires. I am sad, because my answer will not confer upon him that happiness that it would were the answer otherwise. I cannot wed his friend; and I know that my answer will sink to the heart of my father—preventing the realization of his fond and sincere hopes. I am sad, dear Howard, because, for the first time in my life, I must act in opposition to the wishes of my father—the noblest of fathers. Dearly as I love him, I cannot consent to what I know is his sincere wish—this union. That Mr. Wing loves me I do not doubt; that he is a noble man, I know; but I cannot wed him. When he nobly lent his aid to save my father, he made not my hand the condition of his noble act. No, it was an act of purest friendship without a second motive. I esteem and respect him, and love him as my father's friend, but I cannot wed him."

"And you shall not, against your wish," uttered a voice at the entrance of the bower, calmly and pleasantly."

"Mr. Wing!" exclaimed the maiden and her lover in a breath; surprised at the sudden and unexpected appearance of him who was the theme of their conversation.

"Forgive me, Miss Wheelock and Mr. Burton, this intrusion," said the gentleman, after a moment's silence. "Strolling past the bower, I heard my name mentioned, and for a moment I listened to your conversation, and made bold to intrude, for which I beg forgiveness. Miss Wheelock, it is my sincere wish that you answer your father concerning that which has been the topic of your conversation as your heart would answer. Answer him without the least regard as to me. Heaven forbid that I should be the means of severing two such fond and loving hearts. Answer your father without reserve: have no fear of causing him one unhappy thought. I should be most happy and proud to call his daughter my bride; but sooner would I die than sacrifice her happiness. I was blind not to perceive that you loved the man at your side; so near your own age, so well worthy of being your husband. I was blind not to see that each of you loved the other with the truest fondest devotion. I am most unhappy to think that I have been, unwittingly, the cause of a moment's unhappiness to you, Miss Wheelock. Mr. Burton, I resign all thoughts of the beauteous Georgiana, the daughter of my much loved friend, and hope to see her ere long your happy wife. Her father will be as happy as myself to witness the union of two so fond and loving, so endeared to each other.

"Since your father has so cruelly cast you off, Mr. Burton, because of your refusal to wed with a woman of his choosing, I shall take the liberty of being to you a father, and I hope a kind one. Like your father, I have a disowned son; but Heaven knows he was not like yourself, a worthy son. He has forfeited every tie that bound me to him as a father; he has forfeited his inheritance. But you henceforth shall be to me as a son. Would to God he were like you, as worthy!"

Mr. Wing spoke with deep emotion; his feelings were bitter and overpowering as he thought of his own unworthy son. He mastered them in a moment, and again spoke.

"You are cast off by a cruel father, Mr. Burton; but let not your disinheritance be the slightest obstacle in the way of your marriage with the daughter of Colonel Wheelock. He has wealth enough for both of you."

"I have enough for both, my daughter and her husband," were the words of Colonel Wheelock, who had stood for a few moments at the entrance of the arbor, and, until he had spoken, unobserved.

"Dear father, you have been playing the eavesdropper," said his daughter, as she sprang towards him, and imprinted upon his manly face a sweet kiss.

"Only a moment, daughter; you will forgive me, will you not?" returned the Colonel, smiling, and bestowing upon his beauteous daughter a kiss for hers.

"Oh, yes, we forgive you this time: be not guilty again, on pain of our displeasure," replied the maiden, playfully chiding her father, striving in vain to keep a serious expression on her face. In a moment she was laughing heartily.

"Colonel Wheelock, my friend," spoke Mr. Wing at this moment, "I wish to make one request of you."

"Name it, my friend."

"It is this: that you give now, upon the spot, your consent to the union of Howard Burton with your dear daughter. You must, my friend."

"If it is their mutual wish, and yours, my friend, they have my free consent," replied Colonel Wheelock, looking somewhat surprised. "Is this your wish, Mr. Wing?"

"It is my sincere wish, Colonel."

"Is it yours, Howard?"

"It is," answered the young man, gazing with rapture at his beautiful betrothed.

"And yours, Georgie?" asked the Colonel, gazing at his daughter, with a sly, laughing expression in his eyes. "Say no, Georgie," said the Colonel, roguishly laughing.

"Yes," she answered, a deep blush mantling her beautiful face.

"Then I yield; you have my full and free consent, my daughter, and you, Howard. I give her to you; you are well worthy each other. Take her, and be happy!" and as the noble-hearted father spoke, he placed his daughter's hand within her lover's, and blessed the happy couple. "You shall live with me, my son and daughter, for I cannot part with my darling Georgiana. Howard, my dear boy! let not your disinheritance cloud for a moment the bright future of your existence. I have wealth enough for us three."

"He weds your daughter, her equal in this world's goods, Colonel Wheelock. Howard Burton is henceforth to me as a son; he shall be my *heir*."

Mr. Wing uttered these words with pride, and warmth, and noble generosity beaming in his countenance; and as he spoke, he took the arm of Colonel Wheelock, and left the arbor, leaving the happy lovers in mute astonishment at his words.

"Noble, generous man!" exclaimed Burton, in the full impulse of his feelings, after recovering from the spell of astonishment that had bound him in silence for a moment. "An hour ago I came here disinherited—a beggar! I have found indeed a noble father, and am no longer a beggar, but heir to untold wealth. And you, my Georgiana, will ere long be my beautiful bride! Oh God! I am indeed happy; too happy."

The young man spoke with deep emotion, and, overcome by his highly-wrought feelings, gave way to the powerful sentiments that swelled in his bosom. With his face upon the neck of the beauteous girl, he wept tears he could no longer restrain. Unable to restrain her emotion, the beautiful and happy girl gave way to tears, and wept with her lover. There in the bower we will leave the weeping lovers, weeping in happiness.

CHAPTER XIV.

THE BRIDAL.

THE bridal night! The bridal night! What pleasant anticipations, bright hopes, fond emotions, are awakened in the mind of the maiden on her bridal night! How indescribable are the raptures of the enamoured soul when comes the nuptial hour! What fluttering joy, what unspeakable delight, palpitates the maiden's heart when she stands at the altar! The fondest hopes are cherished in her heart, the brightest visions of the future flit through her mind, as at the altar she gazes fondly on him she is to wed; to whose existence she irrevocably joins hers.

A blissful hour to the happy maiden is the nuptial hour! And cursed be he who forgets the marriage vow; who blasts the bright anticipations, the fondly-cherished hopes of the trusting maiden!

*   *   *   *   *   *

There was a brilliant throng gathering in the mansion of Colonel Wheelock; a glittering throng, with smiling, happy faces. There were beauteous maidens in costly attire, and fair dames; gallant lovers, fond husbands, and brothers, all mingled together in the happy throng. Music, sweet swelling music, resounded throughout the mansion; now swelling rich and high its enlivening strains; now in soft, sweet strains, it floated over the scene, the low, rich cadence thrilling to the very soul; now causing the eye to brighten, the cheek to glow, the chest to heave, with its thrilling, richly-swelling strains; now quelling the fire of the eye, softening the glow of the cheek, calming the heaving chest, enchaining all in breathless rapture, with its low, sweet cadence. It was the bridal night of the beauteous Georgiana, the peerless maid of her Highland Home! Peerless she moved amid the brilliant throng that crowded the splendor-robed apartments—among the beautiful, the most beautiful. The queen-star of the scene was the lovely Georgiana!

It was the bridal hour. She stood beside him she loved—the loved one whom she was to wed. Beside him to whom she had given her hand and heart at the altar, beside her affianced, she stood in all her transcendent beauty. Her tall form, towering to its queenly height, its matchless symmetry and grace, the voluptuous beauty of her swelling bust, the tapering waist, the angelic beauty of her face, all combined, enchained the senses in deepest admiration. Every eye was bent in admiring gaze upon the peerless maiden, as she stood beside her affianced, awaiting the bridal ceremony.

She was robed in a dress of costly snow-white satin, the rich gloss flashing in the brilliant light of the apartment like a surface of purest silver. It was an elegant, costly robe, enveloping a form of match-less beauty. The dark hair of the maiden, glossy as silk, fell in ringlets to her swan-like neck and shoulders, that outvied in fairness the Parian marble. Her shoulders, so beautiful and rounded in their outline, so clear, so fair, so roseate, so enchanting to the eye. Her arms, so round, so exquisite in their contour, were bared from little above the elbow; how beautiful their shape! how fair! how clear! how roseate! An exquisitely-turned wrist, and hand so small, so faultless in its form! How ravishing the beauty of her rounded arm, exquisitely-formed hand, and fingers so long and tapering. And her face, how beautiful! how expressive of her heart's happiness! Her fine, high brow, of alabaster white-ness; her dark, beautifully arching eyebrows; her eyes, so dark, so lustrous, so expressive of her inmost soul; how glorious! How adding to the beauty of her eyes were those long, curving lashes, black as midnight's darkest hue! Her nose of the Grecian cast, beautifully formed. Those lips, so small, so rich, so ripe and full, slightly parting, revealed their pearly lining, her teeth, so glittering white, dividing those red, ripe, luscious lips. Her chin, how rounded, how full and beautiful! and her neck, how graceful! Her bosom, so clear, so fair, so dazzling white, swelling and sinking alternately, in its voluptuous beauty! Oh, beautiful, peerlessly beautiful, was the queenly Georgiana, attired in her bridal dress!

Beside her, his tall, elegant form clothed in a rich suit of black, save a snowy vest, stood her lover. His handsome, manly face was marked with a happy pride, as he gazed with fond rapture and admiration at the beauteous maiden.

It was the bridal hour. The man of God was there, and from him ascended a prayer to the throne of Heaven. The prayer was ended. He stood before that bridal pair, so happy, so well matched in beauty, on whom every eye was rivetted in admiration, to perform the marriage ceremony—to make one that happy pair. It is a happy moment, and interesting. Every one of that full company stand in breathless silence, their admiring gaze fixed upon the happy lovers, whom the solemn man of God is about to pronounce man and wife.

A few short moments of breathless silence, and the ceremony was over; Georgiana stood a blushing bride! Now, friends step forward to congratulate the fair bride and happy husband. But ah! what fearful sound is that, that bursts so suddenly upon the ear, appalling every soul of that gay marriage party, so startling the sound? It is a fearful sound, as of crackling flames!

"The mansion is on fire! save yourselves! save

yourselves!" was the wild exclamation of Colonel Wheelock.

Those fearful words, so startling, thrilled with horror the soul of every one of that throng. Wild shrieks burst from the terror-stricken females—wild, agonizing shrieks of alarm. Those faces, so lately flushed with happiness, now are paled to the hue of death, with wild terror. Now, in their wild alarm, they rush from that room, quickly, to escape from the burning house!

Fiercer and more terrible grew the crackling sound : now the fierce red flame burst into the open casements, as they climbed the mansion outside in their rapid, fearful fury. Upward and upward mount the lurid flames, wreathing that beautiful structure in a mantle of fire and destruction. Upward mount the flames to the roof, and shoot into the air their red tongues, like fiery serpents. A few short moments, and the mansion, the beautiful Highland Home, is enveloped in the red ruin! How the high Heavens glow in the red light of the burning mansion ; how crimson their hue! Fiercer grows the heat, higher mount the flames, and ruddier are the Heavens! Sadly gazing upon the flaming mass stand that company in the garden—a sad throng, so lately all happiness! Sad are the faces of that bridal company, as in groups they stand gazing upon the flame-wrapped mansion, so lately a structure of splendor, now a flaming ruin!

"Georgiana! Georgiana! where are you?" cried her father, as he came toward a group, he being the last to leave the burning house.

"Georgiana!" he called loudly, as he passed from one group to another in the garden.

"My daughter! where is she?" he asked, in a tone somewhat of alarm, as he traversed the garden with rapid strides.

"Georgiana! Howard!" he again and again loudly called, in tones of wild apprehension. But there was no answering call from either his daughter or her husband.

"Oh God! where are they?" he cried, wildly. "Did they escape? Yes, yes, I saw them leave myself! but where are they?" and again and again he called loudly their names. Still no answer.

"Look for them! look for them!" he cried to those around, on whose faces fear and apprehension were now seated. "Ha, the bower! they must be there. It is their favorite resort—they must be there, and safe!"

As he spoke these words, in a tone so widely different from the moment before, a tone joyful in its accents, he dashed into the walk that led to the bower, followed by the whole company, anxious and excited.

A cry of surprise and horror came to those behind in a moment, and they beheld the father bend to the earth, near the entrance of the bower, as the cry smote their ears. In an instant they were beside him, and to their horror they beheld, stretched upon the ground, the form of Howard Burton. He lay there senseless, his face gory with blood that streamed from his temple. Surprise and indignation were depicted upon every countenance at the sight.

The bower was entered, but the bride was not there. Her name was called loudly, but no answer came back. Fear for her safety was manifested in the faces of all. Fears they dared not express crowded upon them, and all were silent; every face was pale with wild alarm.

"What means this outrage?" cried Colonel Wheelock, as he raised the inanimate form of Burton from the ground to a sitting posture. "What means this? My daughter, is she there?" he asked, in a tone that trembled from fear.

None could answer him—none could answer that father, "No!" But in their faces he read the answer that rent his soul with agony. "Oh, God! what means this mystery, this outrage? My daughter! Oh, where is my Georgiana?"

His tone was of heart-rending agony, and pierced to the soul of every one with its accents so piteous. My daughter! my daughter!" he wildly cried, in his heart's agony, and he wrung his hands and paced rapidly to and fro in his wild grief. Oh, God! I see it. It is the work of foul villains!" he suddenly exclaimed, in a tone indignant and loud. "They have set fire to my house! My daughter! Oh, God! they have borne her away! Oh, Heaven! is this so? My daughter, my beloved Georgiana, torn away from her home, her father, and her husband, on her wedding night! Oh! the thought is madness; more than I can bear." The tone of the distracted father was agonizing.

Rapidly he paced up and down the fire-lit walk, calling wildly his daughter's name. The agony, the fear that rent his heart, were indescribable. His grief wrought him to distraction. In a voice of frenzy, he called his daughter's name; vainly he called, no daughter answered. Wild and overpowering was the father's grief, the strong man wept bitter, burning tears. Nor in that company around, was there an eye that was not moistened—all were affected to tears.

Vainly his friends strove to soothe the grief of the father : he would not be calm. How piteously he called upon his daughter; how he smote his forehead in his frenzy of grief! It was a sad finale to the wedding—sad indeed. The beautiful mansion wrapped in flames, the bride gone none knew whither, the bridegroom nearly murdered, the father distracted with wildest grief for the loss of his daughter, whose fate he feared the worst, for whom he wildly raved. Sad had the bridal terminated; all that a little while before was sunshine and happiness, was now changed into sorrow and gloom.

The insensible form of Burton was conveyed to a

neighboring mansion, where every possible care and means were taken to bring him to consciousness. The garden was searched all around, and the grounds bordering upon it, but an hour's search proved ineffectual. The object of the anxious search was nowhere to be discovered; the mysterious disappearance of the bride diffused a deep sorrow into the hearts of all.

The grief of the father was without bounds; wildly he raved, and caused the hearts of all to bleed with anguish, so distracted was he in his bereavement.

"Oh, find my daughter! for God's sake, find my Georgiana!" he exclaimed piteously, and he smote his massive forehead, and tore his hair in his soul's agony.

But we will leave the distressed father and his sorrowing friends for other scenes.

On the second day following, near the hour of sunset, the privateer "White Cloud" entered the harbor of Boston. Upon her quarter-deck stood her captain and lieutenant, Wing and Mardon.

"You shall have her, Mardon, if I can get for myself the sister of Marshall. Were it not for her, I should not have entered this port. His sister I must have, and will have before I leave this port. She must be mine. If I get her, you have Burton's fair bride. Ha! ha! a happy bridal, that. Ha! ha! as soon as wedded, to have his bride torn from him. Ha! ha! Howard Burton, I have revenge on you to my heart's content! and to-night I must have Marshall's sister, and that shall be my revenge on him. I will go below and see our fair captive; I love to look at the weeping beauty. To think she is Burton's bride, and in my power, is sweeter revenge than ever I anticipated. Anchor the brigantine off Copp's Hill, Mardon."

As he spoke this to the officer, Wing descended the companion-way, and entered the cabin.

On the very night that Burton was to wed the daughter of Col. Wheelock, the brigantine entered the harbor of New York. Wing immediately proceeded to the residence of his father, and there learned of the wedding. He also learned that his father had disinherited him; that Burton was to be his heir. Maddened and burning for revenge, he left the house with hellish thoughts burning in his breast. He swore to be revenged both upon his father and upon Burton, whom he had no doubt was the instrument of his disinheritance. He resolved to be deeply revenged upon both, by the execution of a devilish plan conceived by him. That plan was to ascend the Hudson to the mansion of Col. Wheelock, and to obtain possession of his daughter by some means or other, and bear her away. Accordingly, with half-a-score of men in a boat, he proceeded up the river. An hour's pulling brought the boat opposite the mansion, which faced the river. Just as the marriage ceremony was about to be performed, Wing fired the mansion in several places, and the flames had strong headway by the time the ceremony was ended. Sending his men back to the boat, he concealed himself to watch for Burton and his bride as they came forth to escape the flames. He saw him rush forth with the half-fainting Georgiana, and hurry with her to the bower. He followed, unobserved; and near the bower he dealt Burton a blow with the butt of a pistol that felled him senseless to the ground. Catching the unhappy bride in his arms, and stifling her cries with one hand pressed firmly upon her mouth, he bore her quickly and unobserved to the boat.

An hour afterwards the brigantine was stretching out of the harbor with the captive bride in the power of the corsair. Wing now resolved to sail for Boston, obtain possession of Marshall's sister, and then leave that port and sail the ocean under the free flag. He had changed the name of the brigantine, and since the night of his robbing the Spanish ship, he had called her "The Witch of the Wave." This name was wrought upon a blood red flag, which for three months had waved aloft.

As the brigantine entered Boston harbor, the second afternoon following the hellish deed consummated by her Captain, the new flag was hauled down, and her former one run up: a broad field of blue with the name "White Cloud" upon it, Wing choosing to run in under this name.

A short time after Wing had entered the cabin, the brigantine came to anchor as he had directed, off Copp's Hill. It was the night we opened our story to the reader, who is already acquainted with its scenes.

THE PIRATE INTERRUPTED.

CHAPTER XV.

THE WITCH OF THE WAVE.

HERE we are, dear reader, where we left you in the second chapter. We did not intend to leave you so long. A pretty way to "tell a tale," we suppose you will say, to begin at the end, and end with the beginning; but we are not quite done.

The reader will recollect what passed in the cabin of the brigantine between the corsair and his captive, who will be recognized as Georgiana Wheelock. He bore her insensible from the cabin to the deck, and getting with her into the boat alongside the brigantine, bade the oarsmen pull away for the pier, where he had twice before landed with other captives, the bound seamen. The boat shot rapidly through the water, and soon touched at the pier. Wing ascended, and his captive was lifted up to him by the men in the boat. The pirate lifted her like a feather in his lion-like strength, and bore her rapidly up the pier through the darkness. Turning into the street in which the "Best Bower" was situated, he strode rapidly on with his burden towards the tap-room. In a few moments he was at the door; it was unfastened and he entered.

"Marshall! Marshall!" he called, but received no answer. All was darkness and silence within. Groping his way to the settee, he placed his inanimate burden upon it, and then opening a door, entered the passage-way that led to the cellar trap. He returned in a moment uttering a volley of oaths.

"By all the fiends of hell! he has set those fellows free!" he exclaimed, in a low, fierce tone of rage, as he returned into the tap-room. Hell's curses on him! He has fairly baulked me in my designs. I have lost his sister, and my revenge! Those fellows will not be likely to keep silence, and I must sail within the hour, or I am snared. You have thwarted me for once, Mike Marshall, but the "Witch of the Wave" will be here again when you little dream of it. I will yet have your sister. I will yet have revenge upon you, as I now have on Burton. He has baulked me, but he shall not escape me!" exclaimed the pirate, fiercely, as he left the tap-room to retrace his way to the boat. He ground his teeth in rage, and muttered oath upon oath as he hurried rapidly towards the pier. Just as he reached it a piercing scream broke the death-like stillness that reigned around. The shriek had proceeded from his captive, who had recovered consciousness, and now struggled to free herself from the pirate with all the strength imparted by despair. But she struggled in vain; her strength gave way, and she gave up in despair. Another wild shriek burst upon the still air, and rang for some seconds around.

"Silence, woman!" said Wing, fiercely. "Another scream, and I will deprive you of that power."

Gathering the struggling woman more closely in his arms, the brutal fiend walked rapidly down the dark pier. Despite his threat his captive uttered another wild shriek of hopeless despair.

"Scream on now, scream on, my fair one; there is none to hear you now," said Wing, in a voice of devilish exultation.

"Halloa there, who screams?" exclaimed a voice in the darkness, near by.

"Oh help me! save me! for God's sake save me!" shrieked the captive, as the voice reached her ear; and a half stifled scream followed her words.

Another instant, and the dark form of a man stood before Wing, and stopped him.

"A woman! what are you doing with her?" said the stranger, sternly. "This is foul violence; let go your hold upon her, villain!"

"And who are you, pray, that speak so imperatively?" said Wing, in a sneering tone.

"Oh save me! for God's sake save me from this man; he is a pirate! Oh save me, save me!" cried the captive, in a beseeching, a heart-rending tone of anguish.

"I will. Let go your hold, I say, man or devil," said the stranger, as he seized hold upon Wing. "Let go your hold upon this woman, or I shall value your life but lightly."

"I will not. Back out of my way, or this dagger shall let your heart's blood forth," said Wing, fiercely enraged, as he drew forth the dagger he had torn from the hand of his captive, in her attempt to take her own life.

He had proceeded but a short distance when he was overtaken by the stranger, who laid strong hold upon him.

"Now yield that woman to my care, or you are a dead man," said the unknown, in a determined tone.

With a violent effort Wing freed himself from the grasp of the stranger, and struck at his breast with the dagger, and again dashed from him. But the blow had missed. The stranger sprang after him, and again seized him. A fierce struggle took place between the two. Wing, a lion in strength, held his captive with his left arm, tightly encircling her waist, while with his right he defended himself. He several times stabbed the stranger, who struggled to throw him to the ground, unmindful of his wounds. For a few seconds they fought fiercely, like tigers; when Wing suddenly exclaimed—

"I'll end this play, and quickly. Halloa! the boat there!" he shouted, loudly. "Halloa the boat!"

"Halloa on shore!" was instantly returned from the boat.

"Help! here, men, quickly."

Hardly a moment elapsed, when half-a-dozen men answered his call for aid. The stranger soon lay senseless upon the ground, and Wing bore the captive, shrieking with the wildest despair, to the boat, followed by his men.

"Let fall, and give way quickly, men. We sail again before sunrise; give way, lively!"

Rapidly the boat shot along the dark waters, and in a few moments lay alongside the brigantine. Wing conveyed his captive, overwhelmed with despairing grief, to the cabin, and returned on deck. He gave orders to slip the cable and make sail, to the no small surprise of the crew, who, however, prepared to execute his command.

"What's in the wind, Captain Wing?" asked Mardon, in some surprise at the orders of the captain.

"Enough! That imp of a devil has set those fellows free. We are betrayed before this; and must get out of the harbor, the quicker the better. Once out to sea, and I defy all chase. We have a good breeze off shore, and will make a quick run out of the harbor. Ha! what is that sound?" exclaimed the pirate, suddenly casting his eyes a-stern. "Mardon, look there, what do you see?" exclaimed he, in a moment after, pointing astern.

"I see two or three boats, and hear the sound of the oars," answered the officer.

"Look! there are three—four—five. I swear there is a dozen of them," said Wing, vehemently, as he counted the boats in the darkness. "By the powers below, this is a narrow escape!" exclaimed Wing. "If we had not slipped our cable we should have been boarded by their crews; for they are out for the brigantine. Look! the boats are pulling rapidly after us."

In the darkness astern, could be discerned the dark forms of the boats, and the sound of oars was distinctly heard as they played in the rowlocks. The brigantine moved slowly through the water, and the boats in pursuit were rapidly gaining upon her.

"Halloa, the brigantine!" shouted a voice from the foremost boat, not twice the length of the brigantine a-stern.

"Ay, ay, the boat!" returned Wing.

"Bring to!" shouted the voice from the boat, commandingly.

"Thank you!" replied Wing, gaily. "I am now under weigh, and don't care about heaving to. She begins to feel the wind more now," he said to his officer, as he glanced aloft at the swelling sails. "Ha, ha! we shall soon laugh at them. See, they do not gain. Pull away, my hearties! I guess you will catch the "Witch of the Wave," he shouted, loudly.

The speed of the brigantine increased momentarily; she glided easily through the dark water, followed by the boats in swift pursuit. They followed swiftly for some moments, but gained not a boat's length upon her. For about fifteen minutes they held on a chase, when the brigantine began to gain, and leave them every moment farther a-stern. Fifteen minutes more, and the boats could not be discerned in the darkness. Swiftly the vessel glided over the dark waters, and as she passed the castle, day began to dawn faintly in the east.

As the sun rose the blood-red flag was run up to the main-mast head, at the command of Wing. Upon it, in letters of gold, was wrought the name of the brigantine. The name wrought in gold flashed in the light of the rising sun like letters of flame.

"That flag henceforth is a free flag!" exclaimed Wing, as it rose and fluttered high aloft its folds of blood-red hue. "A flag that wars on every other that floats; and the name it bears shall yet become the terror of the Atlantic. The "Witch of the Wave" shall be the feared, the dreaded of the seas."

The pirate spoke in deep tones, and his words were sealed with an oath. His eyes flashed beneath his fierce brow, with this wild resolve; and shot forth fiendish glances. He paced the deck for a few moments, and the expression of the face, which was demoniac, would have well become Satan himself.

Suddenly he darted down the companion-way and entered the cabin. Upon the couch laid the captive bride, motionless as one bereft of life. Her face was hidden, as it rested in her hands upon the arms of the couch, by the luxuriant tresses of her dark hair that fell in clustering ringlets from her superbly-shaped head, around her graceful neck, to her bridal robe of snowy satin.

As the pirate entered the cabin, the captive started from her reclining posture, and threw back the dark, abundant tresses of her hair, and gazed with a look of fear at the intruder. It was a look of fear—a look of despair. Her face was pale and wan from two days and nights incessant grief and suffering. Pale as death's most fearful hue, and wan, yet oh, how beautiful!

The pirate gazed at her for a few seconds with admiration. His dark and fearful eyes were fixed upon her, and the fire of hell gleamed forth from them as he gazed. At length he spoke words couched in a dissembling tone of kindness.

"Your grief is violent, my fair one. Grieve no longer, lady; no harm shall come to you. Drive away the sorrow that clouds thy fair face, and smile. I would give the world to see a smile upon thy pretty lips. By my soul! thy spirit will flee from its fair tenement if you much longer burden it with such a heavy weight of grief. Smile, will you not, once?"

The grief-bowed captive gazed at him for a moment, and then spoke.

"Smile," she said, bitterly, and in a tone of sorrow,

"smile! Ask the mother to smile when she lays her fond child in the cold grave! Ask a child to smile, when it gazes upon a mother cold in death! Ask them to smile; if they will, then will I. Aye, ask the sun to give its light in the time of night. Ask the lightnings to leap across the sky when no cloud obscures it—in fair sunshine. Ask the winds to cease; the tempest to still its wrath! If they will do thy bidding, then ask her whom you have torn from her home to smile, and she will!"

Bitterly spoke the sorrowing woman in her grief. Bitter were her words, as they came from her heart bursting with sorrow.

"You liken your smiles to impossibilities, my fair one," said Wing, in a light tone, as he gazed at her, his eyes flashing with lustful admiration. "But come, my pretty one, with me on deck. It is a lovely, invigorating morn, and it would be better to walk the deck for an hour, enjoying the fine sea-breeze, than to be shut up in this cabin."

The captive cast at him a withering glance of scorn and contempt.

"I prefer to remain here," she said, in a firm tone. "Your presence is torture to me in my sorrow. Oh, leave me, leave me to my thoughts, if you have one ray of pity."

Her manner and tone were deeply imploring, and her glorious dark eyes filled to overflowing with tears that coursed down her marble-like face, and rolled upon her snowy robe of satin-like glittering pearls.

"By heaven, she is beautiful!" exclaimed the pirate as he gazed at the weeping woman, his eyes blazing with the lustful passion within him. "Beauti-ful! She is mine. Ha, ha!" he laughed to himself; "this is sweet revenge, Burton—your bride, my mistress!"

There was a look of fiendish gratification expressed in his passion-fired countenance as he spoke, and had the weeping captive but seen his face for that instant, all hopes of mercy would have fled from her bosom, torn with the keenest agony at her fearful situation.

At that instant his name was called from the companion-way by the first officer. He immediately left the cabin for the deck. As he came up and walked forward, Mardon directed his attention towards a topsail schooner bearing down upon the larboard bow of the brigantine, and within gunshot.

"That fellow by his actions appears very anxious to know who we are," said Mardon, speaking of the schooner. "When I first discovered him, he was standing directly for the harbour; but he soon bore up for us, and has been coming down at a cracking rate."

"She is a smart sailer. Get me a glass, Mardon, I want to see if she carries any dogs upon her deck."

The glass was handed him, and he swung himself into the fore-rigging and levelled it at the schooner. He gazed for a few moments through the glass, when he muttered to himself, in a tone of delight,—

"By the powers below! it is *him*. Ha, ha! I will have *him* also in my power! The schooner is unarmed, and he is mine."

He swung himself to the deck, and ordered the fore-topsail to be laid aback. The order was quickly obeyed, and the brigantine, brought to, lay lightly rocking on the waves.

CHAPTER XVI.

THE REVENGE.

THE despairing grief, the heart-rending agony of young Burton, when he recovered to consciousness, and learned of the mysterious disappearance of his fair, new-made bride, may be better imagined by the reader than here described. He was inconsolable, and the more so as neither he nor any other could divine her fate. None could guess respecting her fate; it was wrapped in fearful mystery.

The morning following the bridal night, Mr. Wing left the unhappy father, the sorrowing husband and friends, for his dwelling in Brooklyn. His heart was full of sorrow, for his much loved and valued friend, Colonel Wheelock, and young Burton, whom he had adopted as a son. As they were unhappy, so was he. The grief of the well nigh heart-broken father, the inconsolable despair of the young husband, pained his heart with the bitterest pangs of sorrow.

He was but a few hours absent, when he returned. His face wore a troubled look as he entered a mansion, situated a short distance from the smoking ruins of what the day before was the splendid Highland Home; and where was the unhappy father and husband?

Upon his arrival at his residence, Mr. Wing had learned that his son had been there the night before, and paid a brief visit. As he learned this, a sudden, dark suspicion flashed through his mind, that his son was the author of the foul deed that had plunged a father, husband, and friends, into the deepest sorrow and most agonizing grief. The thought caused his heart the bitterest pangs; and he returned with a heart heavier with sorrow than when he left. Bitter indeed were the feelings, keen the anguish of his soul. To Colonel Wheelock he communicated the dark suspicions concerning his son.

"Great God! can you entertain the thought?" exclaimed he, in the fulness of his heart.

"I do; though it be a bitter thought to me. When I heard this morn that he had been there, after two years' absence, the dark suspicion shot like fire through my brain. I cannot drive it hence; the more I give it thought, the more am I impressed with the belief."

"God forbid it is he that has done this!" exclaimed Colonel Wheelock, as he grasped the hand of his friend. "God forbid! May you be spared this, my friend! It cannot be him; he could have had no motive for the doing of this. No, no, it is not your son. Let not that thought embitter your soul, my dear friend."

Mr. Wing shook his head mournfully, and replied, "I am convinced it must be him, none other. That he is wicked enough for the commission of this deed I am certain. As to motive, he had at least one—revenge."

"Revenge! on whom?"

"Burton and myself. Upon Burton, because of what took place on board the 'Chesapeake.' He was whipped, and to Burton he ascribes the disgrace. He swore revenge upon him, though another officer and not Burton was the means of his punishment. Revenge on me, because he learned last night that I had disowned him. He also learned that it was Burton's wedding night. Colonel Wheelock, it is he who has done this. I would stake my soul upon it."

Mr. Wing uttered these words in a confident tone, that assured his friend that he had not a doubt of the certainty of what he uttered. Both were wrapped in sad and painful silence for a number of minutes, when Mr. Wing broke the silence.

"Colonel Wheelock, we must go to Boston, and learn if the 'White Cloud' has been there. There is a vessel to sail for that port this afternoon, and we must go. We can do so quicker than by land."

"We will go; shall I name to Burton your suspicions?"

"Yes, tell him all; he shall accompany us."

About three hours after the above conversation, Colonel Wheelock, Mr. Wing, and young Burton stood on the quarter-deck of a schooner bound out of the bay of New York. The countenance of each indicated their deep and painful solicitude; the agony that rent their bosoms was plainly written upon their pale and anxious features. The second morning following, the schooner was off Boston harbour. Colonel Wheelock and young Burton were pacing the deck in silent communion with their sad thoughts. Their faces betrayed the keenest anguish and most intense suffering of mind. Mr. Wing was standing forward gazing intently at a sail a-head. He had stood for half an hour with his gaze fixed upon the distant sail, when he suddenly called to Colonel Wheelock, who, with Burton, immediately stood by him.

"Colonel Wheelock, that is the 'White Cloud,'" said Mr. Wing, pointing to the sail. It was a brigantine, and about three miles distant from the schooner, off the larboard bow. She was sailing on a course opposite, but nearly parallel to that of the schooner. "That is the 'White Cloud,' Colonel; I saw her when she sailed from Boston on her first cruise, and I know her. I must get the Captain to bear down upon her and speak her." As Mr. Wing said these words he walked aft to where the Captain stood.

In a few moments the schooner's course was altered, and she stood directly for the brigantine.

"Ha, she has hove to with her fore-topsail aback," said the Captain of the schooner, as he gazed at the brigantine. "You have mistaken her name, sir," he said to Mr. Wing. "Her flag says her name is the 'Witch of the Wave,'" he said, pointing to the red flag that floated from the mainmast head of the brigantine.

"Her name has been changed then," said Mr. Wing. "She is none other than the 'White Cloud.' But why has she hove to?"

"We shall soon know, sir. We shall be within speaking distance in five minutes," said the Captain.

The schooner sped on towards the brigantine that lay motionless upon the waves, and in a few moments was within hailing distance, when the Captain hailed—

"Halloa! the brigantine."

"Ay, ay! the schooner," was returned.

"Was your vessel once called the 'White Cloud?'" asked the Captain of the schooner, as the two vessels now lay alongside each other.

"That was her name, but she now bears another," said the corsair Wing, as he stepped aboard the schooner.

"Ha, my dear father, this meeting is unexpected. I am extremely happy to see you," said the pirate son to his father, in a tone of sarcastic irony. "Ha, my dear Burton, this you? It is a long time since I have seen you, yet I should never have forgotten you. You remember me, I suppose?"

"I do," calmly replied Burton.

"And ever will," said Wing, while the fire of deadly hatred gleamed forth from his eyes.

"I would ask you a few questions, sir," said Mr. Wing, as he stepped to where his son stood. His face and tone were severe.

"Ask on, pray," said the latter, "I will answer all you have to ask." As he spoke he folded his arms across his breast, and looked his father in the face, while a smile of peculiar significance wreathed his lips. It was the smile of a fiend, and to his lips it gave a devilish expression.

"Have you been in New York lately?" asked his father.

"Three nights since, I was there."

"At my house?"

"At *your* house."

"Do you know aught concerning Colonel Wheelock's daughter, sir?" asked the father, sternly.

"If you mean Burton's wife, I do," answered the pirate, in a cool, revengeful tone, while that demon smile yet played upon his lip.

"You do! Then where is she, villain?" exclaimed Burton, vehemently, as he sprang forward and seized hold of Wing.

"In my cabin," said Wing, in a revengeful, scornful tone. "Your bride is my captive, Howard Burton."

As the pirate uttered these words, Burton, with superhuman strength, hurled him to the deck, and on the instant sprang over the bulwarks of the two vessels to the deck of the brigantine.

He sprang down the companion-way, and burst into the cabin, which rang the next instant with a wild cry of delight, as his bride sprang into his arms.

Oh, Howard, dearest Howard, I am saved!" she exclaimed, wild with joy at the deliverance she thought at hand. "Heaven be praised! You have saved me, Howard. But how came you here? Where are we? Oh, take me from here."

"Yes, yes, you are saved; follow me, quickly," said Burton; and as he spoke he left the cabin and ascended the companion-way with his bride.

As they gained the deck an exclamation of horror escaped the lips of Burton. The schooner was twice her length astern of the brigantine. The two vessels had parted.

"Ha, ha, ha!" laughed Wing—a laugh of demoniac exultation. "*You* likewise are my prisoner, Howard Burton."

"Your prisoner; and why, villain?" sharply demanded Burton. "Why is this lady and myself subjected to this treatment, sir pirate, for you deserve no other term? I demand her release and mine."

"And I must comply, I suppose," said Wing, in a sneering tone of irony. "No, no, Howard Burton, you and your bride are in my power, and I will do with you as I will. Think ye I have forgotten the blows I received on your account. No! I swore revenge, and I have it now within my grasp."

"I am in your power; do with me as you will, but in Heaven's name harm not my bride."

"You would invoke pity for her? Did you have pity for me when the lash tortured me? Did you pity me when the blood streamed from the wounds inflicted by the lash? No! you gazed at me with gratified looks: you was glad at heart at my disgrace. Shall I pity you now? My pity is revenge! and you shall feel it."

The pirate spoke in a bitter, revengeful voice, and he gazed at his captives with a look of fiendish delight.

"Willard Wing, with your punishment I had nought to do. You perpetrated upon me an act mean and despicable, such as none who possessed the least honor would have been guilty of. I was aware it was your doing, though you thought I was not. But I did not betray you to punishment. Who it was that informed of you I know not. When I knew you were to be punished, I interceded for you with Captain Lawrence, but he would not hear me, and his sentence was executed upon you."

"And think you, I believe that?" said Wing, in a bitter tone.

"Believe it or not, it is the truth. I offered it not in palliation, or because I feared you. For myself, I beg no mercy from you; but for her, I beg you, in God's name, harm her not, and if you have a human heart you will not."

"You need waste no more words, Howard Burton; ye are both mine."

"We are in your power, and from you I expect any wrong; but may your soul, with the curse of God upon it, for ever suffer the fiercest torments of hell if you harm her. By the Heaven above, if I thought you intended her wrong, you should die upon the spot. For this foul outrage you will yet suffer; your vessel will be pursued and captured, and you will meet with a just punishment."

"Oh, do not enrage him, Howard!" said his wife in a tone of fear, as she clung to him, trembling with terror, her face overspread with a death-like pallor. "Oh, say no more!"

"You talk of capture, Howard Burton," said the pirate, with a sneer. "Know you, there is not a craft that floats that can ride in the wake of the 'Witch of the Wave.' She may be pursued, but never overtaken. Do not flatter yourself that my vessel will be captured; you will be doomed to disappointment if you dream I shall be overtaken. Come, my dove, you will return to the cabin," he said to the trembling bride, and he approached as if to take her from Burton.

"Do not pollute her with thy touch, monster!" said Burton, as he placed himself to shield his wife from the approach of the pirate.

"She must go below, however," said Wing.

"She can go without your aid; I will go with her."

"But you cannot go, sir," said the pirate.

"You shall not part me from her except I part with life." As Burton spoke he drew forth a pistol, and instantly it was levelled at the head of the pirate.

"Go down quickly, Georgiana, to the cabin," he said to his wife, half fainting with terror. She descended the companion-way, while he immediately after descended backwards, his pistol still aimed at the pirate's face, who stood immoveable upon the deck. He gained the cabin, and fastened the door.

"The man that attempts to enter here lies a corpse on the threshold," he exclaimed, with settled determination, as he drew forth another pistol, and laid the two upon the round table, adorned with a top of purest white marble.

At that instant the sound of a voice was heard at the door of the cabin outside. It was the voice of Wing.

"You shall stay there, Howard Burton, you and your bride, till hunger and thirst drive ye forth. Ha! ha! ye shall starve, I say!" and a laugh burst from the lips of the fiend—a laugh of terrible revenge.

"We will starve together ere we will ask relief of a monster like thou," said Burton, a moment after. He seated himself upon the couch beside his terror-stricken bride, and strove to allay her agonizing fears.

CHAPTER XVII.

THE PURSUIT.

AFTER the brigantine had parted from the schooner, the latter held on her course for Boston harbor, which she entered an hour afterwards. About half-an-hour after she came to anchor, an armed brig that had lain at anchor in the stream for two days, left her moorings, and stood out of the bay with every sail spread to a stiff northwester. She was about two hundred tons burden, and of a build that denoted speed. Her hull was black, with no relief. Her masts were very lofty, and her yards square as those of a man-of-war. She carried twelve fourteen pounders, and a long forty-two a-midships. Her decks were white as the driven snow, from the use of the "holy-stone" and sand. The brig was called the "Greyhound," and was a privateer, and had two days before returned to port, after a most successful cruise. She was owned by those who owned the "White Cloud," or now the "Witch of the Wave," and was now bound out of the bay in pursuit of the latter vessel.

Upon her quarter-deck were several gentlemen, among whom was Colonel Wheelock and Mr. Wing. They were conversing respecting the brigantine, and the piratical deeds of her captain and crew.

Forward upon the forecastle, among the crew, was Marshall, the keeper of the tap-room. The reader will recollect what passed between him and the Captain of the brigantine the night previous. After Wing had left him, he remained for some time in the state of surprise and trepidation into which he had been thrown by the words of the pirate, but at length recovered.

What Wing had whispered to him was concerning the female he had seen him stab in a street in New York, and which we have before recounted. He had supposed there was no witness to what he had done, and to him it was the most inexplicable mystery as to how Wing became acquainted with the secret. The woman whom he had stabbed was a poor creature of the town, who had dogged him for an hour, and accosted him a number of times, till he, unable to get rid of her, and irritated beyond all bearing, drew forth a dirk and plunged it in her bosom, when she fell, severely though not mortally wounded; and he, supposing she was dead, fled, and the next morning shipped on board the "Chesapeake."

After he had recovered from his surprise, he for some time deliberated whether or not to liberate the prisoners in his cellar. His desire for revenge upon Wing for his base design upon his sister prompted him to free the prisoners, and to deliver Wing into the power of the law, but the fear of being himself exposed by him deterred him; yet the desire for revenge burned within him, and at length overcame the fear of exposure, and he resolved to run the risk, and liberate the seamen, which he accordingly did, and learned from them all concerning the cruise of the brigantine.

With them he repaired to the residence of one of the owners of the privateer, and hastily made known the particulars of the last cruise, and the scenes of that night. A boat was immediately obtained, and the party put off for the "Greyhound," that lay moored in the stream. Here several other boats were obtained and manned, and made for where the brigantine had anchored, but the bird was on the wing.

After the fruitless chase, the boats returned to the "Greyhound." The owners resolved that the brig, a very fast sailer, should pursue the brigantine; and when the morn broke, they prepared to get her ready for sea. She had received some damage during an action with an East Indiaman, which she had captured and brought to port; and her owners, undecided whether to send her out again as a privateer, had not yet repaired her.

At sunrise the work of repairing the damage was commenced, and in three hours was finished, and the brig ready for sea. It was about the hour of nine when the New York schooner came to anchor, within pistol shot of the armed brig. Mr. Wing had seen upon her deck the owners of the brigantine, and wishing to speak with them, was with Col. Wheelock rowed off to the brig.

He met them with a sad heart and sad countenance, and to them related the abduction of Col. Wheelock's daughter by his son; in what way he had obtained possession of her, and of the retention of her husband on board the brigantine, where both were now captives. He related all to them, and learned to his great joy that the brig was then getting ready for the pursuit, and he and Colonel Wheelock resolved to remain on board. We have seen the "Greyhound" under weigh, standing out of the harbor, with her towering pyramids of canvass swelling with the wind, and filled to their utmost tension. Swiftly and gallantly she bounded over the flashing waters, and seemed gifted with the matchless speed of the animal from which she derived her name. Colonel Wheelock paced the deck, wrapped in the deepest melancholy. His fine features were haggard, from the agony that racked his breast. At times his thoughts dwelt upon the speedy restoration of his daughter safe to his arms, and on this hope he dwelt with joy. But then again, as he thought of her dreadful situation, as he thought of her in the power of a pirate, a fiend in human form, all hope died within him; and the misery, the agony, the despair of the grief-stricken father seemed more than he could bear.

No less miserable was Mr. Wing, as thought of his son, now a fugitive, a pirate. Bitter and painful were the thoughts that crowded his brain. Though he had cast him off—disinherited him, yet he was his son, his own and only son; and bitter were the pangs that shot through his breast at the thoughts. But as he thought, he grew stern, and he prayed within him that his son might be taken, and suffer the punishment his crimes so well merited.

The course of the brig after she left the harbor was shaped southerly, the direction the brigantine had sailed. Though the brigantine had several hours the start, yet the Captain of the "Greyhound" expressed confidence in his being able to bring the former vessel within sight ere nightfall, if she continued upon the same course.

The gallant "Greyhound" dashed swiftly on over the waves of blue, at a speed that seemed impossible to rival. She held on till the sun had passed the meridian; on, with undiminishing speed, till the sun was sinking in the western arch of azure.

The blazing orb was an hour high, when from the look-out of the brig came the cry of—

"Sail, ho!"

"Where away?" demanded the Captain.

"Right a-head," returned the look-out.

In the distant horizon a-head could be discerned a white speck, like a snowy sea-gull in the distance. The Captain levelled a glass at the distant sail, and for some time his gaze was fixed steadily upon it.

"Can you make it out, Captain?" asked a young man, the lieutenant, as the Captain took the glass from his eye.

"No, it is too far distant. Bet a bottle of wine it is the brigantine," said the Captain, in a confident tone. "We must keep a sharp look-out throughout the night, and by morning we may be able to make her out."

The "Greyhound" continued on her course during the night; swiftly she ploughed through the dark waters; swiftly she was borne onward, with every sail tightened to its utmost stretch. A sharp watch had been kept with night-glasses for the sail that had been discovered, and when the morn broke upon the ocean, it was found that the brig had gained upon it. She kept swiftly on during the whole day, and at the hour of sunset, the distant sail was made out by the aid of the glass a brigantine; and all on board were satisfied that it was the "Witch of the Wave." On, throughout the night, the "Greyhound" bounded over the dark ocean, at a speed that seemed to rival the wind; and when the day dawned, the brigantine was plainly made out without the aid of a glass.

"That is the brigantine, gentlemen," said the Captain of the brig, addressing four gentlemen who stood upon the forecastle, two of the owners of the brig, and Colonel Wheelock and Mr. Wing.

"She will hear the howl of the "Greyhound" ere many hours. I bet a bottle of wine it was her when I first saw her but a speck in the distance. Suppose we go below and drink to her speedy capture, gentlemen?"

At his suggestion they repaired with him to the cabin, and drank to the capture of the brigantine and her piratical crew, and returned again on deck. On dashed the brig, and it was evident she gained every moment upon the brigantine, till mid-day, when the two vessels were not more than four miles apart.

"We gain upon her nobly," said the Captain to his lieutenant; "by sunset we will show her the 'Greyhound's' teeth."

On over the flashing waves dashed the brig, in swift pursuit of the brigantine, that flew before her with a speed that it seemed impossible to excel.

On dashed the pursuer and the pursued till the sun was dipping in the blue ocean, when the lieutenant of the brig said to the captain—

"We have not gained an inch since noon, Captain Wilder; not an inch, and I doubt if we have held our own."

"We have held our own, Keating, but have not gained, that is certain," said the Captain to his lieutenant. "She does sail, though. If she beats the 'Greyhound' at sailing, and escapes, she is rightly named the 'Witch of the Wave;' but, Keating, she shall not escape the 'Greyhound.' I will throw overboard six of our guns to-night, and that will lighten us considerably. The brigantine carries ten, but the brig will match her with six guns.

DEATH OF THE PIRATE.

Besides, we have twenty men more than her complement, and those twelve who were so roughly used, will be apt to fight some, I reckon. We have a cracking wind, but I wish it would blow harder."

"The brigantine would not sail any faster, I suppose?" said the lieutenant, laughing.

"I only thought of the brig," returned the Captain. "It is sunset now; as soon as it is dark, we will over with six of our guns."

As the Captain spoke, he walked aft to where stood Colonel Wheelock, Mr. Wing, and the other two gentlemen, owners of the brig.

CHAPTER XVIII.

THE FIGHT.

THE sun had gone down behind a barrier of clouds that stretched along the western horizon, gorgeous with the hues of purple and gold. But the bright sunset soon faded, and darkness settled upon the deep.

Two hours after sunset the brig was dashing on with accelerated speed. She had been lightened of six of her guns, three on each side, forward, and her speed was considerably increased. It was midnight when the Captain, who had been scanning the brigantine with his night glass, said to his lieutenant that the brig was gaining on the chase.

"I will go below now, Keating. You take this glass, and keep watch on the brigantine. Call me at eight bells." As the Captain spoke he went below.

The brig dashed on till four o'clock, when eight bells were struck, and the Captain was called from below. During the last four hours the brig had gained on the brigantine, and the two vessels were now not more than two miles apart. The Captain, as he came on deck, took his night glass and levelled it at the chase.

"We have gained on her, and are gaining fast," he said.

At sunrise the distance between the two vessels was lessened one half, and the brig was gaining fast. On she bounded in chase, like a hound upon the scent.

"One hour more, and I will hail her!" said the Captain. "Dash on, my gallant 'Greyhound,' your prey is before you!" said he, in a lively tone.

For an hour the two vessels flew on, and were now within hailing distance; the brig off the starboard quarter of the brigantine, and gaining every instant. A few moments, and the two vessels were right a-beam, and within pistol shot.

"We have had a long race, and you have got beaten!" shouted Captain Wilder to Wing, who stood by the starboard bulwarks, on the quarter-deck of the brigantine.

"For the first time!" returned Wing. "What brig is that?"

"The 'Greyhound,' from Boston, on a cruise!" answered Captain Wilder.

"It is the first craft that ever outsailed the 'Witch of the Wave!'" said Wing. "When did you sail from Boston?" he asked.

"A week since."

"Was there a privateer there called the 'White Cloud?'"

"Not when we sailed; she was expected in soon," returned Captain Wilder. "And will be, I reckon," he said to himself. "But here's luck to the 'Witch of the Wave!' the 'Greyhound' is leaving her!" he shouted a moment after to Wing. "The fellow don't mistrust us; he thinks this merely a race. Ha, ha! capital, that! I'll astonish him a little. Starboard the helm a little," he said to the helmsman, in a low tone, as he stood near him. "That will do."

The brig was about twice her length a-head of the other when the Captain gave his order, and, as she stood now, threatened to run afoul of the brigantine.

"Halloa there, lubbers! you will be afoul of us!" shouted Wing.

"Oh, no; no danger," said Captain Wilder, carelessly.

"No, I should think not," said Wing. "Starboard the helm, hard up!" he shouted to his helmsman.

His order was obeyed, but too late; the brigantine was struck on the starboard bow by the brig, and in a moment the two vessels lay locked yard-arm and yard-arm. A moment, and the brig's crew were pouring upon the deck of the brigantine, all armed and prepared for a deadly conflict.

The crew of the brigantine were taken by surprise, but were all armed; for Wing had expected an attack from the brig, and had ordered his men to get ready for a fight. He had supposed that the brig had been in chase of him, and expected an attack from her guns. But he had been deceived by the conversation between him and Captain Wilder, and supposed then that the brig had fallen in with him by chance, and that the pursuit had been merely a trial of speed.

Nor was he undeceived till the brig run afoul of his vessel, and poured her crew upon his decks. He was fairly surprised; but he soon recovered, and, with a drawn cutlass, he sprang forward from where he had stood, by the helm, to meet the foe. It was but a moment ere the crews of both vessels were engaged in fierce and deadly contest. The ringing and clashing of steel opposing steel—the sharp, incessant report of pistols—the wild shouts of the combatants engaged in terrible strife—the groans and yells of agony of the wounded, were all blended wildly together in the wild harmony of battle.

The pirates were driven aft the mainmast by the crew of the brig, and there made their stand, and with their Captain at their head, fought like devils. The privateersmen pressed hotly upon them, and fought as fiercely. Superior in numbers, and as well trained to battle, the odds were greatly in their favor.

Fierce and terrible was the bloody contest; the deck of the brigantine became slippery with gore, and was strewn with dead and dying. A score and a half of the pirates lay dead or in the agonies of death upon the deck, and half that number of privateersmen.

"At them, boys! Death to the pirates!" shouted Captain Wilder to his men, and they pressed upon the pirates with terrible slaughter, and thinned their numbers every moment, till they cried for quarter.

"Cowards! damnable cowards! Do you cry for quarter?" shouted Wing, mad with rage and fury. "The gibbet will be the only quarter they will give ye! Do ye ask it? Cowards! Would ye rather die upon the gibbet than here? I die here! Follow me, who will!"

As he spoke, he sprang with his upraised cutlass into the ranks of the privateersmen, followed by all his men, inspired with new courage by his words. The onset was terrible; fearful the clash of steel; terrific the reports of pistols; wild the yells that rang upon the air! The pirates fought desperately and with terrible fury. The privateersmen gave way before them, and were driven to the forecastle, when their Captain shouted to them to stand, and yield no farther.

The strife raged for a short time with fearful fury upon the forecastle; the privateersmen fought bravely against their savage foe, though it seemed for a few short moments that two of their number fell to one of the foe. Yet they fought on, unflinchingly; and now they gain! they press hotly upon the foe, who retreat inch by inch, fighting with fiercest fury, to the quarter-deck.

At the moment the pirates, in their terrible charge, had driven the privateersmen forward, and left the quarter-deck, the form of a man sprang up the companion-way—it was Burton. He gazed for a moment at the combatants, and then descended to the cabin. Upon the couch reclined his wife, the beautiful Georgiana, half dead with hunger, and thirst, and fear. Burton sprang towards her, and raised her from the couch.

"Come, dearest Georgiana, quickly; we are saved!" he said, as he supported her to the companion-way. She was too weak to ascend, and he, mustering all his strength, bore her in his arms to the deck. The strife was yet raging upon the forecastle, and the dread sounds of battle struck terror to the soul of Burton's wife.

"Have no fears! you are saved, my Georgiana!" exclaimed the fond husband, as he reached the deck.

He sprang from the companion-way to the bulwarks, and in another moment stood with his bride upon the quarter-deck. He quickly descended to the cabin, where were Colonel Wheelock and Mr. Wing.

"My daughter! my daughter! my son!" exclaimed Colonel Wheelock, as he sprang up.

"My father; my father!" murmured his daughter, and she fell fainting into his arms.

"You are safe, my Georgiana; and you, Howard, my son. Thank God! thank God! you are safe, both," exclaimed the father, with fervent joy—joy, without bounds.

Mr. Wing grasped the hands of young Burton, and expressed the most unbounded joy at his safety. It was a happy moment.

But we will return on deck. We left the pirates retreating from the forecastle before the privateersmen, who pressed upon them, dealing terrible slaughter around. Slowly the pirates retreated, fighting like demons. Inch by inch they gave way till the fierce contest raged upon the quarter-deck. The voices of the two captains could be heard encouraging their men in the deadly strife. Fierce and deadly was the contest upon the quarter-deck for a few short moments, when the pirates yielded, seeing that death to the whole of them was inevitable if they continued the battle. They laid down their arms and again asked quarter.

"Hold, men!" shouted Captain Wilder. "Strike not another blow. The foe has struck; the day is ours. Retire to the cabin quickly, and see to the captives there; release them!" he said to his lieutenant.

The young officer instantly descended the companion-way in obedience to the command. Immediately after him sprang down Wing, his cutlass dripping with gore. There was a terrible fire in his eye, and in his face a terrific expression. Captain Wilder, fearing he would interfere with his officer, instantly followed him.

At the foot of the companion-way Wing raised a trap, and drawing forth from his belt a pistol, cocked it, and pointed the muzzle to the dark space at his feet. A terrible smile wreathed his lips as he stood thus and gazed at the Captain of the brig who stood in the companion-way. It was a smile of fearful triumph.

"Captain Wilder, you are the victor in this contest; my men have yielded to you, but I have not, nor will I. I have yet the command of this vessel, and of the lives of all on board of her. Captain Wilder, I give you five minutes, and but five, to leave the deck of this vessel for your own, with your men: or, at a movement of my finger, I launch you all into dark eternity."

The pirate spoke in a deep tone of fearful determination, and his eyes flashed like fire coals beneath his fierce brow.

"This is my magazine, the rear is filled with powder; a movement of my finger and the brigantine and all on board of her are doomed."

"You involve yourself in the common destruction if you fire the magazine," said Captain Wilder.

"Ha, ha, ha! and which do you think I prefer—a death like this, or a death on the gibbet? But I have no more to say. One minute of the five has expired."

The pirate remained for a moment silent, and the expression of his face was one of stern and terrible determination, as he stood with his pistol pointing to the magazine.

Captain Wilder read in the face of the pirate the terrible resolve of his soul, and he called to his officer, who stood behind the pirate at the entrance of the cabin.

"Stay a moment, Captain Wilder, I have other conditions. Swear that you will molest me no further in pursuit, or with your guns. Swear, or you cannot leave."

The Captain gazed into the face of the pirate, and read the fearful determination of his soul, and he knew that he must yield.

"I swear to molest you no further," Capt. Wilder said. "But where is Burton and his wife?" he asked of his officer.

"Not in the cabin," replied the officer.

"Where are they?" he asked of Wing.

"If they are not in the cabin they have escaped. I know not where they are. But two minutes of the five are left, Captain Wilder," said the pirate, looking at his watch.

The next instant the Captain of the brig and his officer were on the deck, and they quickly ordered their men to the brig. The crew quickly obeyed the order, and before two minutes had expired, the two vessels had parted. As soon as he gained the deck of the brig, the Captain descended to the cabin, where, to his inexpressible satisfaction, he beheld young Burton and his wife in safety.

After the two vessels had parted, Wing came on deck and ordered it to be cleared of the dead that lay strewn around. Half his crew had been killed in the fight, and lay in their gore upon the deck. The remainder fell to work at his command to clear the deck.

Wing walked forward to the mainmast, near which lay half-a-dozen of his men dead. Suddenly he ejaculated with surprise—

"By Heaven! there lies Mike Marshall—dead!" and as he spoke these words he turned over the bulky form of Mike with his feet.

"No, I ain't dead yet, Will Wing!" exclaimed Mike, who sprang to his feet, and stood before the pirate, who seemed utterly confounded at seeing him he had thought dead rise up before him.

Mike clutched a pistol in his hand, thrust the muzzle to the face of Wing, and fired. Simultaneously with the report came a wild yell of agony, and the pirate fell a corpse to the deck! He lay dead, a horrible sight to the eye. Not a feature of his face was distinguishable; his head was a shattered, shapeless mass. It was a terrible end to his checquered and eventful life. As Mike fired, he sprang across the deck, and over the bulwarks into the sea, but he received a dozen pistol bullets in his body, and he sunk to his grave in the ocean.

After the 'Greyhound' had parted from the brigantine, her course was laid for Boston, and in half an hour she had sailed out of sight of the brigantine, and at the end of three days arrived at Boston. The day following she departed again and sailed for New York, having on board Colonel Wheelock, Mr. Wing, Howard Burton, and his wife—four of the happiest of human beings. They arrived safely at New York, and repaired to the city residence of Colonel Wheelock.

A year afterwards Mr. Wing died, causing his friends the deepest sorrow. He bequeathed to Burton nearly all his immense wealth, and died blessing him and his lovely wife.

Colonel Wheelock lived to a good old age. Burton and his Georgiana are yet living; and since their escape from the piratical brigantine have lived in the enjoyment of every earthly happiness.

One year from the departure of the 'Witch of the Wave' from Boston, she was heard from as cruising in the Mediterranean. She became a terror to that sea; she was feared by all who sailed those waters. Mardon was her commander, and he scoured the Mediterranean for a year under the free flag, when his vessel was captured by a French cruiser, and he and all his crew were executed.

LONDON: W. S. JOHNSON, "NASSAU STEAM PRESS," 60, ST. MARTIN'S LANE.